PURRFECT GAME

THE MYSTERIES OF MAX 55

NIC SAINT

PURRFECT GAME

The Mysteries of Max 55

Copyright © 2022 by Nic Saint

All rights reserved. No part of this book may be reproduced in any form by any electronic or mechanical means including photocopying, recording, or information storage and retrieval without permission in writing from the author.

This is a work of fiction. Names, characters, places, brands, media, and incidents are either the product of the author's imagination or are used fictitiously. The author acknowledges the trademarked status and trademark owners of various products referenced in this work of fiction, which have been used without permission. The publication/use of these trademarks is not authorized, associated with, or sponsored by the trademark owners.

Edited by Chereese Graves

www.nicsaint.com

Give feedback on the book at: info@nicsaint.com

facebook.com/nicsaintauthor
@nicsaintauthor

First Edition

Printed in the U.S.A

PURRFECT GAME

Game, Set and Murder

For some reason I find hard to understand, humans like to play a game called tennis. Basically it involves hitting a ball with something called a racket and inducing it to fly across a net. The person on the other side then proceeds to hit the ball back across that same net. And so on and so forth, ad infinitum. Or at least until someone strikes out, and the other person wins the set, or even the game, and eventually the match.

It's all very complicated, and not all that interesting, not to say utterly boring, and so when Marge and Tex went on their annual tennis retreat with some of their friends from the tennis club, I mainly saw this as an opportunity to catch up on my naptime, which had suffered greatly since my humans had decided to produce a new human in the form of a baby. Unfortunately for them, before long a murder was committed, and suspicion fell on all those present—Marge and Tex included!

And then of course there was Gran acting strange—

which isn't all that exceptional, considering strange is that eccentric old lady's middle name—and Harriet acting even stranger, with Brutus convinced she was having an affair. In other words: I had my work cut out for me, trying to unravel everyone's secrets and their most blatant lies.

CHAPTER 1

Sometimes Marge wondered what it would be like to play with a different partner than her husband Tex. Not that Tex was a bad tennis player, per se, but it could hardly be said that he was a good one either. Even though Tex never failed to mention that he was trained by the great Pete Sampras himself, and had acquired a degree from the highly respected Ross School Tennis Academy, this enviable pedigree didn't show in his game, which was fair to middling at best.

The couple were enjoying the annual tennis extravaganza organized by Michele Droba, prominent socialite and fellow member of the Riviera Country Club. As Michele saw it, this was simply a fun week spent amongst friends and tennis fans, and the Pooles had been welcome guests for going on fifteen years now. At the moment they were playing a doubles game against Vena and Glenn Aleman, the veterinarian and her bookseller husband. And it had to be said that in spite of Tex's self-proclaimed tennis prowess, Vena and Glenn were winning.

As usual, Michele had rented an Airbnb on the outskirts of Hampton Cove, the town where they all lived, and this year had brought in a new person in the form of Ona Konpacka, the retired supermodel, who was accompanied by new beau Max Stinger, the well-known plastic surgeon. Rumor had it that Ona's face had been disfigured to such an extent in a botched procedure that it had ended her illustrious modeling career, and that it was only through the genius talent of the brilliant Max Stinger that her famous features had been restored to some extent.

And it was true that Ona once more looked more or less like her old self. Even though her modeling days were behind her once and for all, at least she was able to leave her apartment again, instead of locking herself in like a recluse. This tennis week was in fact one of the first social occasions for the former model—and so far things were looking well. Ona had written a book about her harrowing experience—*From Heaven to Hell and Back Again*—and it had quickly captured the imagination of the nation and was now a certified number-one bestseller.

Vena fired off another zinger and Tex, trying to return it, stumbled and fell, soiling his perfectly nice tennis shorts and cursing under his breath. An amiable man under normal circumstances, the doctor displayed a fierce competitive streak when he hit the tennis court. Not John McEnroe level stuff, but still.

"Relax, Tex," said Marge when her husband shot a distinctly nasty glance across the court in the direction of their opponents, who were exchanging a high five. "It's just a friendly game."

"She did that on purpose," Tex grumbled. "Always aiming for the body."

"Vena wasn't aiming for the body," said Marge as she watched the veterinarian getting ready to serve.

"Not Vena—Glenn! He's always playing dirty."

"I don't think so," said Marge as she followed Vena's movements like a hawk.

"Oh, yes, he does."

"Shush, honey," said Marge, "and focus."

It was true, of course, that Glenn Aleman suffered from the same competitive proclivity as Tex, which had caused some fireworks on the court in the past few days. But playing dirty? Nah. They were all friends here, and nobody wanted to risk that friendship just so they could score the winning point.

A loud thwack sounded and the ball came zooming in Marge's direction at considerable speed. Vena might only be a couple of years younger than Marge, but she had power. Which was par for the course if you extracted foals from horses and calves from cows. With some effort, Marge managed to return Vena's serve. The vet quickly approached the net, though, and performed a stunning volley, sending the ball hurtling in Tex's direction at speed. The doctor, taken by surprise, was unable to respond in kind. Instead he hit the ball with the shaft of his tennis racket. The ball ricocheted and shot into the air, then landed on top of Tex's head.

"Game, set and match to the Alemans!" Michele shouted. Their hostess was acting as the game's umpire, and took this responsibility seriously. "Well done, Vena and Glenn! Great game, you two. And well played, Marge and Tex!"

"Great game, my foot," Tex said as he hit the air with his racket a couple of times in an attempt to vent his righteous anger.

"They won fair and square, honey," said Marge. "Now shake hands."

"I won't shake hands with a cheater," Tex muttered angrily.

"Shake hands, Tex," Marge insisted. "Don't be a sore loser."

"Oh, all right," said Tex as he joined his wife at the net. They shook hands with their opponents, Tex in a halfhearted sort of way, and that was that.

"Well played, buddy," said Glenn Aleman, as he clapped the doctor on the back. "Better luck next time, huh."

"I guess," said Tex.

"You did good," said Vena, addressing Marge. "Your game has really improved."

"You think so?" said Marge. "I have been working hard on my backhand."

"I can tell. Keep this up and you'll become a most formidable opponent." The vet lowered her voice. "Is everything all right with your husband? He looks upset."

"Tex doesn't like to lose," said Marge as she grabbed a towel and draped it across her neck. "Even though by now he should be used to it." It was true that they hadn't won a single game since they'd arrived at the house.

"Maybe we have to let him win a couple of times?" Vena suggested.

"Oh, no. He has to win fair and square."

"Just to improve his mood?"

"Out of the question."

"Though admittedly Glenn would rather die than throw a game. He's such a mild-mannered man, always sweet-tempered, but put a tennis racket in his hands and he turns into some kind of psycho maniac. Has to win at all cost."

"Same thing with Tex. Once he's on the court he thinks he's Novak Djokovic."

And as the two ladies discussed their husbands' strange quirks, Glenn invited Tex for a drink. And even though the two men had just been ready to drink each other's blood, now that the game had been decided, they mysteriously morphed back into their customary amiable selves, and soon were chatting pleasantly.

CHAPTER 2

Relieved from her task as umpire, Michele Droba returned to the conversation she'd been engaged in with her boyfriend Christopher Bonarowski. She still felt odd about calling him her boyfriend, even though of course he was. At some point they might have to make things official, but she wasn't sure how her kids would respond. It was seven years now since she lost her husband Dean, but Michael and Drew still missed their dad. They liked Chris, but didn't exactly adore him. Then again, she wasn't absolutely sure *she* adored him. She was fond of him, of course, as he was such a wonderful man—erudite and knowledgeable and oh, so very affectionate, never stinting on compliments and little attentions. It was nice to be adored by such an important man—respected as a publisher and very, very successful. But love? She wasn't even sure what the word meant. She had once loved her husband, or at least she thought she had. But that was a long time ago.

"So have you seen the manuscript?" she asked, picking up their conversation where they left off. "Has Isobel even shown it to you yet?"

"Not yet," said Chris as he quickly checked something on his phone. "She says it's not ready yet, and she wants the thing to be ready before she shows it to anyone—even me, her publisher."

"Can't you talk her out of it? I mean, there must be something you can do."

Chris put his phone down and gave her a quizzical look. "We discussed this, Michele. You know your sister-in-law. Once she has her mind set on something, there's no talking her out of it. In that sense she's just like you."

She bridled to some extent. "I hope I'm not as unreasonable as Isobel. In fact I know I'm not. And I would never humiliate my friends the way she's doing."

"I'm sure that's not her intention. And whatever she writes will have to be vetted by me before it's even published. So there's nothing to worry about."

"Easy for you to say. You won't be in the book."

"How do you know? Maybe she's devoting an entire chapter to me."

"I very much doubt it," said Michele as she smoothed her pristinely white tennis shirt, then tucked her long blond tresses behind her ears. In her mid-forties, she had retained the figure of her teenage years, and even her face was still relatively wrinkle-free, much to the envy of her female friends, who often wondered how she did it. "Otherwise she would have told you. Like she told me, and the rest of our circle of friends."

"Look, I can assure you that by the time Isobel's autobiography goes out, there won't be anything controversial left in the text. You have my word on that." He patted her knee affectionately. "There's nothing to worry about, sweetheart. Nothing at all." He gave her a reassuring smile. He might be a full decade older than she was, but he still looked youthful enough to pass as her contemporary. But then he spent much of his leisure time playing tennis, and not on long drawn-out lunches or games of golf as a lot of his colleagues did.

"Mh."

In spite of Chris's reassurances, Michele was still worried. She knew Isobel, and what she had told her had given her great cause for concern. When Isobel's husband Gavin had disappeared seven years ago, it had led to a complete meltdown and had precipitated the most dreadful episode in Isobel's life. It had taken years and countless sessions of counseling before Michele's sister-in-law had managed to extricate herself from the claws of the alcohol demon and take control of her life again. She still attended regular AA meetings, which is where she'd picked up the idea to write a book about her life, detailing her own descent into madness, and revealing the truth about what happened to her.

Not content with sharing her own secrets, though, she was now so enamored with the notion of cleansing her life by shining a light on all that was dark and shameful that she had decided to extend this treatment to all her loved ones. When she had announced to Michele what it was that she intended to do, Michele was shocked. But arguing with Isobel had proven useless: the woman was so convinced she was doing the right thing that it was impossible to talk her out of it.

At least she'd accepted Michele's suggestion to bring her project to Chris, who might be able to subject the autobiography to an editor's eagle-eyed scrutiny and weed out the most egregious problems before being unleashed upon the world.

"Look, it's all part of Isobel's process," said Chris, repeating a mantra he'd been using ever since they'd signed the contract for the book. "And you have to admit that she's doing much better since she started writing her autobiography."

"Of course it's her process," Michele agreed, "but why does she have to drag us into it? She can write about herself all she wants, but not about me or the kids."

"I'm sure she'll keep Michael and Drew out of it," said Chris.

"I should hope so. Though she should keep us all out of it."

"I'm afraid that ship has sailed," said Chris, and returned to checking his messages.

Michele gave him a sideways glance. Chris came at this from a different angle than she did, of course. For him this autobiography meant a great deal of money. Dean and Gavin Droba were the sons of Bill Droba, of Droba Group fame. The Droba tires were renowned around the world, and had made the Droba family very rich indeed. Even the tragedy that had befallen them seven years ago hadn't managed to put a dent into this success story, and so when a member of the family had announced a tell-all autobiography, speculation was rife, and already the press had been peppering them with questions. According to Chris sales figures for Isobel's autobiography might even exceed those of political luminaries like Bill Clinton or Barack Obama, who had sold millions of their life stories.

Millions upon millions of people—reading saucy stories about their personal lives. For a private person like Michele this was nothing short of a nightmare.

CHAPTER 3

*O*na Konpacka took great precautions to protect her precious skin from the sun. Not only had she selected the biggest umbrella for herself, but she was also wearing a long-sleeved shirt, cotton pants, outsized sunglasses, and lathered the parts of her skin that were exposed in a thick layer of sunscreen at regular intervals.

Once the best-paid model on the planet, an incompetent plastic surgeon had ended her career when he'd injected her face and parts of her body with fillers that had triggered the most horrendous allergic reaction, causing her famous face and figure to become disfigured. Only through the diligent and patient ministrations of genius cosmetic surgeon Max Stinger had the damage been undone. She would never be a model again, but at least she looked human again, and was able to leave her apartment, after locking herself up like a recluse for the best part of the past two years. Max had earned her eternal gratitude, and model and surgeon had grown so close during this period that they'd become a couple.

"Are you sure I should be out here?" she asked for the

gazillionth time. "Everyone knows that scar tissue shouldn't be exposed to the sun, right?"

Max, who was reading the latest Patterson, didn't look up. "You're not in the sun, sugar plum. You're in the shade. Nothing to worry about."

Now that she had her looks back—or at least partly—she wasn't taking any chances. Which was why she wasn't playing any matches. No singles and no doubles. She'd made this clear to Michele, who hadn't hesitated to invite her anyway.

She was grateful to Michele, one of the few people who had kept in touch after the incident, and had been a great support in the year she'd been terrified that she would never look like herself again.

Her miniature Brussels Griffon Joey jumped on her lap, and she tickled the doggie behind the ears. Then a second Brussels Griffon followed the first when Zoey joined Joey. Michele had told her a couple of weeks ago that it wasn't a good idea for a little doggie like Joey to be alone, and didn't she want to get her precious darling a friend? And that's how Zoey had come into their lives. Now both her constant companions, she loved the two doggies with all her heart. In fact if it hadn't been for them, she didn't know how she would have survived.

She hugged both sweethearts to her chest, and giggled when they licked her face—they soon stopped though. Probably didn't like the taste of sunscreen!

🐾

*M*arge was heading upstairs to take a shower after her doubles match when she heard noises of a fight in progress. She was passing by the room where Isobel Droba was staying, and if she wasn't mistaken the voice raised in anger was that of Isobel's daughter Alison. For a moment Marge dawdled on the doorstep, pressing her ear to the door. She wasn't normally one for peeking through keyholes or listening at doors, but this business between Isobel and her daughter had been going on for a while now, and it frankly worried her a great deal.

"You can't do this!" Alison was saying.

"Watch me," Isobel returned coldly.

"You're such a—"

"Hey! Watch your language, young lady!"

Marge shook her head. Even though Alison wasn't a teenager anymore, her volcanic temper still persisted to this day. For as long as Marge could remember mother and daughter had been having arguments. Sometimes about things as mundane as a skirt Alison had bought that her mom thought too short, or a new car Alison felt she was entitled to. But recently the arguments had turned even more acrimonious. Ever since Alison had met a young man named Jason Rocamora, in fact. Alison had had boyfriends before, of course, and some of them hadn't met her mother's approval. But Jason was an ex-con, and when that little fact had been brought to Isobel's attention, she'd blown a gasket, and had forbidden her daughter to keep seeing this highly unsuitable suitor.

But Alison wasn't a kid anymore. She was twenty-one, and had told her mom in no uncertain terms what she could do with her opinions about Jason.

"Look, Mom," said Alison in measured tones. "I'm going to marry Jason whether you like it or not. And if you want to cut me off financially, so be it."

"Honey, can't you see that Jason is all wrong for you? He's a criminal!"

"Ex-criminal, Mom. And besides, he was wrongfully convicted."

"That's what they all say."

"In his case it's true."

"Of course it is."

"God, Mom!" Alison exploded. "You're simply impossible!"

Marge heard the stomping of footsteps coming in her direction, and quickly removed her ear from the door and herself further along the corridor. Moments later the door was yanked open and Alison came storming out. She didn't even see Marge, too busy as she was fuming over her mother's refusal to back her betrothal.

"Alison, come back here!" Isobel shouted as she, too, appeared in the corridor.

But her daughter was already stomping down the stairs. Isobel blinked when she saw Marge.

"Hi," said Marge, feeling a little embarrassed.

"Hi," said Isobel, rearranging her features into a weak smile. "Teenagers," she said, rolling her eyes. "Always something."

"Tell me about it," said Marge.

The two women stood there for a moment, in awkward silence, then Isobel turned on her heel and strode back into her room, gently closing the door.

Tex came up the stairs, mounting them two at a time. He must have caught the tail end of the incident, for he asked, "I heard shouting. What was that all about?"

"Alison wants to get married," said Marge, "but her mom doesn't approve."

"She wants to *marry* the guy now?" said Tex, who was fully *au courant* of the whole Jason Rocamora drama, as was the rest of the guests at the house.

"Looks like. Isobel said she'll cut her off if she goes through with the wedding."

"Tough," said Tex. He glanced at the closed door. "Maybe we should intervene?"

"I don't think so," said Marge. "Best to stay out of this."

"Yeah, I guess," said Tex, looking quietly relieved.

Much to their detriment they had learned that sometimes the best way to lose a friend was to get involved in their personal business. Isobel might think they were taking sides. And besides, if she wanted their advice, she would have asked for it. As it was, she might simply take offense if they tried to intervene.

It was in moments like these that she thanked her lucky stars that they'd always maintained such a good relationship with their own daughter. And that when Odelia had arrived home one day to deliver a fiancé on the mat, it had been a cop and not a criminal. Reformed as Jason Rocamora might be, he still sounded like bad news. And it was with this thought that they entered their own room for a much-needed shower.

CHAPTER 4

*P*erlita Gruner was in the bedroom she shared with her husband, putting sunscreen on her face and getting ready for their doubles match. A handsome woman in her early fifties with an abundance of flaming red hair, she was nevertheless concerned about a suspicious-looking spot that had appeared on her face in recent weeks. And as she studied herself in the vanity mirror, she wondered whether to make an appointment with a dermatologist to have it checked out. According to Nathan it was just a mole, but moles could be tricky.

She lifted her chin and saw to her satisfaction that the skin wasn't as saggy as it could have been. Especially now, she wanted to look her absolute best. She had even wondered if she should accept Michele's invitation this year or not. With so much going on in her life she didn't want to be stuck in a house for a week. But then she'd remembered that these people were her friends, and that she always felt so uplifted at the end of the sojourn, and had decided to come after all.

Her phone chimed and she glanced in the direction of the

bathroom door, where Nathan had been ensconced for the past twenty minutes, and quickly grabbed her phone. When she read the message she smiled, then replied. And she'd just finished deleting the message when her husband walked out of the bathroom, a towel wrapped around his midsection, hair wet from his shower.

"Most people take a shower after the match," she said as she finished rubbing the creamy substance on her face and neck, taking care not to skip her ears.

"Yeah, well, I like to take a shower before and after," said Nathan as he cut a glance to his phone, which was lying on the bed. "Makes me feel refreshed." A tall man a few years her senior, he looked fit and healthy, which was a boon in his line of work. As a successful art dealer, he was mingling with the movers and shakers of the art world on a daily basis, people who put a premium on beauty and good looks. "Have you heard from Izzy?"

Perlita shook her head. "I'm going to have Dr. Blumberg take a look at this mole," she said.

"Oh, for God's sakes, Perlita. It's just a mole."

"I don't like it. I want it gone." It was her face, after all. This mole had no business popping up uninvited. "I'm sure Dr. Blumberg will know what to do."

"Fine," Nathan murmured as he picked up his phone and stared at it for a moment, looking puzzled. "So no word from Izzy?"

"I'm sure everything is fine, Nate."

"I guess so."

Izzy Price was the promising young artist the couple had taken under their wing. Nathan was representing her business interests, while Perlita, who owned the Gruner Gallery in downtown Hampton Cove, was organizing the young artist's first-ever exhibition in two months. Perlita had commissioned three dozen paintings from Izzy, but so far she had only finished the first dozen, which gave Nathan cause for concern. In spite of his long association with artists—or maybe because of it—he habitually fretted about their capacity to deliver on command. And since Izzy had never completed such a big order before, he wondered if they hadn't jumped the gun and offered her this opportunity before she was ready. That they might burn her out and end her career before it even got started.

"You know what Izzy is like," she said. "She performs well under pressure."

"Let's hope she does. Two dozen paintings in two months is a lot."

Perlita got up, grabbed her towel and water bottle and headed for the door. "Ready?" she asked.

"Just give me a minute," said Nathan as he picked up his phone. That frown was still cutting his brow.

She sighed and walked out. "Don't be late, Nate."

"Mh."

⁂

The moment his wife had left, Nathan tiptoed to the door and listened intently. Satisfied that she was gone, he dialed the number. When a female voice purred in his ear, his frown disappeared and immediately a warm smile crept up his face.

"Are you sure Perlita doesn't know?" she asked.

"Absolutely. She doesn't have a clue."

"When will I see you, Nate?"

"Soon—I promise."

"Why did you have to go to this tennis thing? And with your wife, no less."

"It's only a week, sweetheart. One more week, and then we'll be together."

"Pinky swear?"

"Scout's honor."

She giggled, a lovely sound. "I can't wait."

Neither could he. The thought of that luscious young body and those flexible limbs made him giddy with desire. "Same here," he said hoarsely.

§

Isobel sat motionless for a moment. The fight with her daughter had affected her more deeply than she would have thought. She hated these fights, but what was the alternative? To give Alison what she wanted? Impossible. Jason Rocamora was bad news. If Alison married him, he would drag her down into the abyss, and destroy her life and her future. She couldn't have that. That marriage must never take place.

Her phone chimed and she picked up immediately. "Yes, any news?"

"She got into Jason's car and they took off," said the voice on the other end. It was the PI she had hired to keep tabs on Jason and her daughter. Mark Devine was an ace at what he did. He was the one who had discovered that Rocamora had a criminal record. That he'd done time for aggravated robbery, and was bad news.

"Focus on Jason," she instructed. "I want you to catch him in something illegal."

"Of course," said Mark, and she could hear that he was driving.

"Are you following them now?"

"Yeah, I'm right behind them. Looks like they're driving to his place."

She nodded thoughtfully, willing herself to stay strong and not to let her imagination run wild. Ever since leaving her mother's home three months ago, after one of their fights, Alison had moved in with Jason, causing Isobel sleepless nights as she lay awake imagining what that horrible man was doing to her little girl. If only Mark could catch Jason in some illegal activity, and inform the police, they might be able to put him in jail again, and end this ill-fated romance. And even if he wasn't up to his usual criminal behavior, Mark or one of his operatives had to be there to protect Alison from this extremely dangerous individual.

She'd already talked to the police, but they said there was nothing they could do, as there was no law against associating with, or getting married to, an ex-con. When she had first discovered Jason's past, she'd been shocked, but also satisfied that Alison would see the light, and break things off with the guy. But instead Alison had told her she knew all about her boyfriend's past, and that he was innocent. Wrongfully accused and wrongfully imprisoned! Clearly he'd gotten under her skin, and was probably laughing his ass off now, getting married to this little rich girl. So she'd decided to cut Alison off if she went through with the wedding. News that Alison hadn't taken too well, but that couldn't be helped.

She just had to make her daughter understand she was doing this for her own good. She was doing this because she loved her, and wanted to protect her.

A curt knock sounded at the door and when it opened Michele walked in.

"Please don't let him out of your sight, Mark," she said, and ended the call.

On the desk, her laptop was open, and immediately Michele's gaze was drawn to it. "Is that it?" she asked. "Is that the manuscript?"

Isobel closed the laptop before her sister-in-law could take a look. "What do you want?" she asked, none too friendly. She didn't have the bandwidth at the moment to deal with Michele's nonsense on top of everything else going on.

"Please, Isobel," said Michele, getting that pleading look in her eyes again. "Won't you reconsider? If you go through with this crazy plan of yours we won't have any friends left. You'll alienate everyone."

"The book is done, Michele," she said. "So there's nothing more to discuss."

"Have you sent it to Chris yet?"

Isobel produced a curt laugh. "He's your boyfriend, why don't you ask him?"

"I have asked him, and he says you haven't delivered the manuscript yet."

"Well, there you go." In spite of herself she felt sorry for her sister-in-law. "Look, this is all for the best, Michele. Secrets and lies are like poison. They fester and kill. Once everything is out in the open, only then can we truly heal ourselves."

"Okay, I understand that to be true for you, but why expose other people's secrets? Can't you see you're causing a great deal of pain and suffering?"

"That's because they haven't lived through what I have. Once they realize how freeing it is to live with the truth, they'll thank me." She spread her arms. "Embrace the truth, Michele. It will set you free."

But Michele didn't look as if she was ready to embrace anything. On the contrary. She was closer to tears than laughter. "Why are you doing this to us?" she wanted to know. "What did we ever do to you?"

"Nothing," said Isobel truthfully. "But I have to do this. It's important to me."

It was all part of the healing process. Once she had exorcised these demons from her past, she could finally breathe.

She could finally live. Oh, how she longed for the day her truth was finally revealed. She knew it would set her free.

"Please think about it," said Michele.

"For the past years I've done nothing *but* think about it," she said quietly. "But this is how it must be, Michele. My mind is made up. Please understand that."

The moment her sister-in-law had left, she slumped in her chair, then buried her face in her hands. Oh, how she wished Gavin was here. He would know what to do about Alison. In fact if Gavin was still here their daughter might never have hooked up with the likes of Jason Rocamora. She was only fourteen when her dad was taken from them. How their lives would have been different if he wasn't.

CHAPTER 5

Odelia and Chase had left for work, and Marge and Tex were enjoying a week-long tennis thing with their friends from the tennis club, and so the house was empty. Apart from myself and Dooley, that is. And I have to say, that's exactly the way I like it. Now, before you go hurling all kinds of silly accusations my way about cats being solitary animals, or even selfish, and that the feline of the species don't care about anyone other than themselves, I would like to state for the record that this cat, in particular, is very fond of his humans. So fond, in fact, that I've managed to stick around for as long as I have. But even cats as keen on his human caretakers as myself need their alone time from time to time. And so I didn't mind that the house was empty, for it allowed me to luxuriate in the abundance of space the absence of two large humans had left on the bed.

"It's so nice to finally have the bed all to ourselves, isn't it, Max?" said Dooley, who wholeheartedly agrees with me on a cat's occasional need for privacy.

"Absolute bliss," I said as I explored the innate softness of

Odelia's pillow while Dooley submitted Chase's pillow to the same treatment, happily kneading it.

"I don't like these ergonomic pillows, though," said Dooley, touching on one minor point of criticism. "They're too hard—and they've got bumps in all the wrong places."

"Chase might argue that the bumps are in all the right places," I murmured. After all, these ergonomic pillows are designed to support the human neck, apparently a very delicate part of the human anatomy, as Chase often complains about something or even someone being a pain in the neck. More often than not this someone might be a criminal he's been pursuing, or a member of the public making his life difficult with outrageous requests, or even a police colleague.

In other words: it's tough to be a human sometimes, having to endure the vicissitudes of life on a daily basis. And especially tough on the human neck.

"Why doesn't Odelia have an ergonomic pillow?" Dooley wanted to know. He'd abandoned his explorations of Chase's pillow and retreated to the comfy duvet Odelia had been so kind to smoothen out for us before she left for work.

Tonight Chase might cavil at the presence of a few hairs on his duvet, but that couldn't be helped. He might even sneeze and rub his face, blaming us for the tickling sensation he experienced, and telling tall tales about cat hair being the bane of his existence, and wouldn't it be a good idea to get a dog instead. But Odelia would soon put him straight. She'd say that if you lie down with dogs, you get up with fleas, and would he prefer big fat fleas to a few teeny tiny hairs?

"I guess Odelia doesn't experience the same kind of pain in the neck her husband does," I said, though I must confess I hadn't given the topic a lot of thought before this moment. "Maybe being a reporter is less taxing on the neck than being a cop?"

"That must be it," Dooley agreed as he finished circling a

favored spot and finally deigned it with his presence. "Odd that *we* never get a pain in the neck, isn't it, Max? I mean, we never use ergonomic pillows and we're always fine."

"That's because the human anatomy is vastly inferior to the feline anatomy," I said. "When God created man he made a few mistakes, which he decided to rectify when he created the feline, which is why cats ended up being a superior species."

"What mistakes?" asked Dooley, curious now.

"Well, the human head weighs about eleven pounds, and all of that weight has to be supported by seven vertebrae and around twenty muscles. That's a lot of weight being brought to bear on the poor neck. Add to that the fact that most people now go through life glancing at their mobile phones on a practically continuous basis, and the pressure increases manyfold." I was warming to my subject now, and felt like a professor standing in front of an auditorium of eager pupils soaking up his wisdom. "When a human holds their head at a forty-five-degree angle the weight on the neck increases to almost fifty pounds."

"That's a lot of weight," Dooley marveled.

"Yeah, it's a miracle humans can still function."

"It's all because of gravity, though, isn't it, Max?"

"Possibly," I said, yawning cavernously.

"If gravity wasn't pulling on them so much they wouldn't need ergonomic pillows or walking sticks or even walkers."

When we were out and about in Hampton Cove the day before, we'd come across an old lady with a walker, which had caused Dooley to marvel at this curious invention.

"True," I admitted.

"I mean, I've never seen a cat with a walker before—have you?"

"No, I can't say that I have," I agreed.

"Must be because we're so much smaller than humans,

and we don't walk upright. And so the forces of gravity affect us a lot less than they do humans."

"Mh," I said, my eyes drooping closed as sleep got ready to envelop me.

"So the obvious solution would be to dial down this gravity thing, Max."

"And how do you suppose we do that?"

"I don't know. But there must be a way. Scientists are clever."

"Not that clever."

"Well, anyway," Dooley insisted stubbornly. "They need to fix this thing, Max. And then Chase wouldn't need this silly pillow of his, with all these funny bumps."

"You can have Odelia's pillow tomorrow," I murmured, correctly surmising that this might be the real issue at stake here, not gravity or the essential frailty of the human neck. I opened one eye to regard my friend. He was smiling at me.

"Thanks, Max," he said with a touch of emotion.

"You're very welcome, buddy."

"We could create a schedule. I could take Odelia's pillow on the even days of the month, and then you could take it on the odd days. What do you say?"

"I say it's a deal," I said sleepily.

This matter laid to rest to our mutual satisfaction, we settled in for the duration. And I'd just descended into the land of dreams, where life is grand and the scent of fried chicken is the *parfum du jour*, when the sound of stomping feet on the stairs told me the house wasn't as fully devoid of life as we'd surmised.

Moments later Gran burst into the room, glanced around with a feverish sort of look on her face, and said, "Have you seen Grace? Where is Grace? Tell me!"

"I have absolutely no idea," I said truthfully. After all, I'm not my human's daughter's keeper. Gran is Grace's designated babysitter on those days when the daycare center is closed—which fortunately for Gran—and Grace—rarely happens. "Isn't she at the daycare center?"

A sort of pensive look stole over Gran's face, then finally a smile spread across those same craggy dales and valleys and she pointed a stubby finger in my direction. "Max, you're absolutely right. Thank God! I thought I lost her!"

And with these words, she stomped out again.

Dooley and I exchanged a puzzled glance.

"Gravity seems to affect Gran's head as much as it affects Chase's neck," Dooley commented.

"You might well be correct, Dooley," I said.

Though it might not be gravity causing Gran to become confused about Grace's whereabouts. At any rate, it was something we clearly needed to bring to Odelia's attention. It's one thing to forget where you put your keys, but quite another when you can't remember where you've put your great-granddaughter.

CHAPTER 6

My peaceful date with Odelia's pillow was once again interrupted when Brutus came sidling into the room. Our butch black friend was acting furtive, and kept looking over his shoulder. Lowering his voice, he said, "Max! I need a word!"

"Grace is at the daycare center," Dooley said. "So you didn't lose her, Brutus."

Brutus gave Dooley an odd look, then hopped onto the bed and whispered, "It's Harriet. She's been acting strange lately!"

I would have told him that he was no stranger in the acting strange department, but decided to hold my tongue. Instead, I said, "What do you mean?"

"Yes, strange how, Brutus?" Dooley asked, intrigued by this news.

"Furtive, if you know what I mean," said Brutus. "Sneaking out of the house at all hours of the day and night, and not telling me where she's going. Giving me weird glances when she thinks I'm not looking."

"What kind of weird glances?" asked Dooley, resting his head on his front paws. "Can you give us an example?"

Brutus looked uncomfortable. It's one thing to describe a glance, but quite another to attempt to recreate it. He now rearranged his features into a sort of constipated look, as if he was having a bowel movement but it hadn't decided yet whether it was coming or going.

"Please don't do doo-doo on the duvet," Dooley said, who'd interpreted the look the same way I had. "Chase might kick us out and get a dog instead."

"I'm not going to doo-doo on the duvet!" said Brutus, dropping the whispery voice he'd been employing. "This is how Harriet has been looking at me."

"Mh," I said, finding it hard to imagine that Harriet, who's a real Persian in every sense of the word, would ever lower herself to looking like this.

"I'm telling you she's harboring some kind of secret," said Brutus. "And I want you guys to find out what it is. Cause she's not telling me, and it's driving me nuts!"

"I think Harriet's secret is probably that she needs to do doo-doo but is unable to," Dooley surmised. "In which case she needs to go and see Vena."

"Can't," I said. "Vena is at that same tennis do with Marge and Tex."

"Tennis doo-doo?" asked Dooley.

"Tennis do, not doo-doo," I clarified.

Dooley laughed. "I thought so! I can't even imagine what a tennis doo-doo would look like! Probably a doo-doo with a yellow streak and fuzz on top!"

I let him enjoy his little joke, then got down to brass tacks. "To be honest I haven't noticed anything strange in Harriet's behavior, Brutus," I said. "But if you want I'll have a word with her. Try and find out what's going on?"

"Oh, would you, Max?" said Brutus, gratitude making his

voice wobbly. "I'm going absolutely crazy with this thing. I keep thinking she's having an affair."

"Now why would Harriet be having an affair?" I said, giving our friend a reassuring pat on the back. "We all know she's crazy about you, buddy."

"I don't know about that. Lately she's been acting very cold. You know, unaffectionate."

"You mean…" I produced a delicate cough. It's one thing to pour your heart out to a friend, but quite another to discuss the intimate details of one's relationship.

"It's been two weeks, three days and six hours, Max," said Brutus sadly.

I coughed again as I directed a discreet glance at Dooley, who was following the conversation with the sort of gleam in his eyes he gets when he finds something exceedingly fascinating. It's the same look he gets when there's a nature documentary on the Discovery Channel he finds of particular interest. Like the one about the dating life of the carpenter ant the other night.

"What's been two weeks, three days and six hours, Brutus?" he asked now.

"Well, um…" said Brutus, darting a nervous look at me. "Um, well…"

"It's been two weeks, three days and six hours since Harriet last ate a piece of chicken," I said. There were probably a million things I could have said, but this was the first thing that came to mind, unfortunately. I blame it on a lack of sleep!

"Harriet is a vegetarian now?" asked Dooley excitedly. "But that's great news! I'm also a vegetarian!"

"No, you're not," I said.

"But of course I am. I never eat meat."

"You have to eat meat, Dooley. You're a carnivore. If you don't eat meat, you die."

"I don't think so. All I eat is kibble and those delicious wet food pouches they give us. And I've asked Odelia and Marge and they've assured me those are one hundred percent vegetarian."

"As if," Brutus murmured with a slight smile, but then was serious again. "I think it's Kingman," he said. "I think Harriet is having an affair with Kingman."

This had me stunned. "Kingman? Are you sure?"

Brutus nodded sadly. "I followed her last night. After we left cat choir? Instead of going straight home, she said she was going for a stroll. So I tailed her."

"And what happened?" I asked.

"She went back to the park, for a midnight meeting with Kingman!"

"Did they... you know?" I asked delicately.

"Nothing untoward happened," he said stiffly. "But that doesn't mean anything. They could be working up to something. And they were standing far too close to each other to my liking, I can tell you that. In fact I came this close to breaking cover and pouncing on the double-crossing swine."

"I didn't know Kingman was a swine," said Dooley, much surprised. "I thought he was a cat. Like us."

"Just a figure of speech, Dooley," I said absentmindedly. If Harriet was holding secret midnight meetings with Kingman in the park, Brutus did indeed have cause for concern. Not unlike his human Wilbur Vickery, Kingman is a well-known Lothario, and can't allow a female feline to pass the General Store, his habitual perch, without giving them the once-over, and more often than not the twice or even third-over. He had always refrained from putting the moves on Harriet, having far too much respect for Brutus—or qualms about the latter's physical prowess and inclination for pugnaciousness —to try. Though it must also be said that Harriet has never fancied Kingman. Brutus has always been the one for her—

or at least he was from the moment the large cat had arrived on the scene.

And now this.

"I'm sorry, Brutus," I said, and I meant it. Theirs had been a fairytale romance, and if it was true what he said, things were going to change around here. Not in the least because Harriet and Brutus lived together. What would happen if Harriet were to move out and move in with Kingman? Great changes.

"I don't like this," said Dooley, who'd finally caught on. "Kingman and Harriet?"

Brutus nodded somberly. "And I'll bet it's Kingman she's been seeing all this time—sneaking out whenever she thinks I'm not looking. It's a terrible thing."

"I don't understand," said Dooley. "Why would Kingman do this to you?"

"Because he can?" Brutus said, hanging his head. I would have told him that inclining the head at a forty-five-degree angle was bad for the neck, but now didn't seem like a good time for a PSA. "Because he's got something I don't have?"

"He's very popular," Dooley allowed.

Brutus snapped his head up. "What's that supposed to mean? I'm popular!"

"Not as popular as Kingman, Brutus," said Dooley, who must not have realized how dangerously close to peril he was coming by stating these simple truths. "Kingman is like the king of Hampton Cove. He's a very popular cat." Brutus made a sort of growling sound at the back of his throat, and his eyes narrowed into slits, tail distending and back arching. I think Dooley must have finally realized his faux-pas, for he quickly added, "But not as popular as you, obviously."

"Yeah, you're very well-liked," I hastened to say.

The size of our friend's tail returned to normal, and he lost some of his pep when he said, "No, you're right, Dooley.

Kingman is a lot more popular than me. He's Mr. Popular. Everybody loves him. And now, apparently, so does Harriet." He heaved a deep sigh that seemed to come from the very depths of his soul. "It's over. That's just how it is. Harriet doesn't love me anymore." And then his spine seemed to turn to jelly and he sort of melted onto the duvet, leaving only the broken husk of what was formerly the most formidable cat I've ever known. Some might even call Brutus a bully, and I know I've used the term myself on occasion, but deep down, underneath that hardened crust, he has a heart of solid gold.

"Cheer up, buddy," I said, putting a paw on his shoulder. "I'll talk to Harriet. Find out her secret. And who knows? Maybe you've got this all wrong."

"I don't think so," he said with a croaky voice. "She's leaving me, Max." He squeezed his eyes firmly shut. "And now please leave me. I would be alone."

And so I offered him Odelia's pillow, and he gladly took it. And as he curled up into a ball, liberally littering the pillow with black fur, Dooley and I took our leave.

We had been tasked with an important mission: to discover whether Harriet's secret meetings with Kingman meant she was having an affair with the latter.

Frankly it was with a heart bowed down with the weight of woe that I set out on this mission. For I had the distinct impression that when we returned from our investigations into the mind of Harriet, we'd be bearing bad tidings for our friend.

CHAPTER 7

We went in search of Harriet and found her in the backyard belonging to the Trappers—Marge and Tex's neighbors. She was chatting with the Trappers' sheepdog Rufus. The two were deep in conversation, but the moment we arrived on the scene, they looked up, and I had the impression we'd caught them discussing something that wasn't intended for our ears.

"What's going on?" I asked therefore.

"Oh, just chatting about this and that," said Harriet breezily.

"Yeah, this and that and that and this," said Rufus, just as airily.

I could have told them they were both lousy liars, for it was obvious that whatever they'd been discussing was important. Harriet's affair with Kingman?

I had intended to tackle the matter with some delicacy—to ease into the discussion gradually, but Dooley had other ideas. "Is it true that you're having an affair with Kingman?" he demanded to know.

Harriet looked shocked. "What?!" she said after a moment.

"You've been sneaking around behind Brutus's back," Dooley explained. "And now he thinks you're having an affair with Kingman, because he saw the two of you together in the park last night."

Harriet made a display of looking completely flabbergasted. "I don't believe what I'm hearing," she said finally. "Of course I'm not having an affair!"

"So what have you been doing sneaking out at all hours of the day or night?"

"Excuse me?"

Dooley took a breath and repeated, "What have you been doing sneaking—"

"I heard you the first time, Dooley," she said with a touch of hauteur. "And for your information, I haven't been sneaking out. And I'm not having an affair."

Dooley frowned. This all sounded highly suspicious. "So what's going on?"

"Nothing is going on! Except that it's obvious to me that my dear Brutus has a highly active imagination."

Harriet had never referred to Brutus in these clinical terms before. Usually it's smoochie poo this and snuggle bunny that, but never 'my dear Brutus.' Something was definitely going on here, Brutus was right about that. But what?

"Okay, so Brutus is worried," I said, deciding to play the sympathy card.

"Look, a girl can have her secrets, can't she?" said Harriet, becoming defensive. "Or don't you two have secrets to hide?"

"I don't have any secrets," I said.

"Me neither," Dooley chimed in.

Harriet threw her head back and produced a tinkling laugh. "As if!" she cried, when she'd finished her hyena act. "We all have secrets. Isn't that so, Rufus?"

Rufus seemed uncomfortable. "Well…" he prevaricated.

"Of course you have," said Harriet. "Like that time you pretended to be someone you were not so you could chat with me. Remember? That was a big secret."

It hadn't been Rufus's finest hour. He'd pretended to be a war veteran, and had connected with Harriet through Pettr, a dating app for pets. "It wasn't exactly a secret," Rufus muttered nervously. "Just… a way to make friends, I guess."

"Or how about you, Max?" said Harriet, turning to me. "Or don't you think I know that you always eat the first scoops of fresh kibble from the bag?"

I stared at her. "You know about that?" I asked, aghast.

"Of course! The moment Marge opens a new bag, or Odelia, you're always quick to gobble up those precious first nuggets."

"They're the freshest," I mumbled, my face flushed with embarrassment. Lucky for me nobody could see just how flushed my face was, what with all the blorange fur covering my shamefaced cheeks.

"I know they're the freshest. Straight out of the bag kibble tastes the best."

It's common knowledge amongst cats that the moment kibble has been lying there for a couple of hours it loses some of that precious flavor and that crunch. And the same goes for bags that have been open for a couple of days or weeks.

"Oh, and how about when they open a fresh bag, and you empty all four bowls in quick succession before the rest of us can even get close?"

"First dibs," I murmured, glancing down to the ground now.

"For a twenty-pound kitty you move pretty fast, Max."

"I don't weigh twenty pounds," I said, glancing up.

"What about my secrets, Harriet?" asked Dooley.

Harriet smiled. "I know for a fact that when Brutus and I first started dating, that you turned our love nest into a lavatory, Dooley," she said. From Dooley's quick intake of breath, it was clear she wasn't lying. "Doo-doo and wee-wee both!"

"I-I'm sorry," Dooley stammered. "I didn't think you knew?"

"How could I not know, Dooley? Don't you think I recognize your scent?"

"I was going through a difficult time," said Dooley, wide-eyed.

"I know," said Harriet, softening. "And it's all right, Dooley."

Like pretty much the entire Hampton Cove male cat contingent, Dooley had once been fervently in love with Harriet. So when she'd given her heart to an outsider in the form of Brutus, he and the rest of Harriet's admirers hadn't been too well pleased. Though I have to admit this business about Dooley doing his business in the rose bushes, where Harriet and Brutus habitually got together, was news to me.

"I'll never do it again," said Dooley quietly.

"I know you'll never do it again," said Harriet. "In fact you haven't done it since. The only reason I brought it up is to show you we all have secrets. And that's fine."

"I guess so," I said finally. "And I guess Brutus has his secrets, too."

Harriet frowned at this. "Brutus doesn't have any secrets from me." Her frown deepened. "Does he?"

"I wouldn't know," I said. "If I did, it wouldn't be a secret, now would it?"

She narrowed her eyes at me. "You know something, don't you, Max?"

"I swear that I don't," I said, holding up my paws in a display of innocence.

"What is Brutus's secret!" she demanded heatedly. "Tell me!"

"But I thought you just said we're all entitled to our secrets?" asked Dooley.

Harriet's face worked. "Fine. Be that way. But don't think this is the end."

And with these words, she stalked off, tail high in the air, and disappeared through the opening in the fence between the two backyards.

I noticed how Rufus was eyeing me with a flicker of mirth in his mellow brown eyes. "You did that on purpose, didn't you, Max?" he said finally.

"Did what on purpose?" I asked innocently.

"Suggesting that Brutus has a secret he hasn't shared with Harriet."

"I have no idea what you're talking about," I said, and gave him a wink.

CHAPTER 8

With all this drama going on, I didn't even have time to have another lie-down on my favorite new spot—Odelia's pillow—until that evening when Brutus finally vacated the premises. But by then Odelia and Chase had returned home, after picking Grace up from daycare, and dinner time rolled around, which involves our humans feeding us first, before feeding themselves—the natural order.

"Is it true that you always eat all four bowls of kibble when Odelia opens a new bag, Max?" asked Dooley as we both tucked into our food.

I nodded, still feeling the sting of shame. "I do that," I admitted. "It's just that the first kibble tastes so delicious, fresh out of the bag. There's simply no substitute." And besides, the moment Odelia finds our bowls empty, or Marge, they fill them up again. "It's one of those small pleasures I like to indulge in," I said.

Though now that my secret was out, I probably wouldn't do it again. Nor would I get the chance, for my housemates would probably come running when they heard the sound of a fresh bag being opened, and I simply wouldn't get the chance! I might not weigh twenty pounds, like Harriet seems to think, but it's true that I'm the big-boned type of feline, and not all that quick off the mark. The only way I've been able to get first dibs is because I keep a close eye on those bags, so I know when a bag is almost empty, and the time has come to open a new one.

"You can eat from my bowl any time, Max," said Dooley magnanimously. "I don't mind."

"Thanks, Dooley," I said, giving my friend a grateful look. "I didn't know that Harriet knew, though."

"I didn't know she knew about me doing my business in those rose bushes," said Dooley. "If I'd known I probably wouldn't have done it."

"Water under the bridge now," I said, my mouth full of delicious wet food.

"Wee-wee under the rose bushes," Dooley murmured thoughtfully. "Do you think it's true, though, what Harriet said? That all cats have secrets?"

"I guess so," I said.

"I wonder what Harriet's secret is."

"Probably that she's having an affair with Kingman."

We were both silent as we ruminated on the consequences of this affair. Brutus was our dear friend, but so was Kingman. But if Harriet shifted her affections from the former to the latter, we might have to choose between the two. Not unlike a couple getting a divorce. They divide their worldly belongings, like the house they shared, or the furniture. But they also end up dividing their friends, since it's hard to stay friends with both, especially if the divorce is acrimonious. I just hoped we wouldn't have to choose between Brutus and Kingman. Though if we had to, we'd probably choose Brutus, since he's the most muscular one of the two of them, and would beat us up if we chose Kingman.

Having fed her cats, Odelia now proceeded to feed Grace, while Chase made inroads in dinner prep for himself and his wife. Gran was also joining us, since she usually ate dinner with her daughter and son-in-law, who were away from home.

I wondered if this was the right moment to broach a delicate subject: the fact that Gran seemed to have forgotten it wasn't her day to take care of Grace. But Odelia and Chase were discussing other matters, so I decided the topic would keep.

"Have you heard from your mom and dad?" asked Chase as he used a wooden spoon to stir some unknown substance on the stove.

"I'll talk to them tonight," said Odelia as she made a valiant attempt to enter food into her daughter's mouth. Grace was seated in her high chair at the table, and seemed to be having a good time, for she was babbling her secret language, presumably addressing people who weren't there—perhaps her friends from the daycare center. "Last time we spoke they seemed to be doing fine."

"Maybe next year we could join them," Chase suggested as he tasted the food he was preparing. Judging from his frown it wasn't up to snuff yet.

"I don't know, Chase," said Odelia. "I'm not much of a tennis player."

"Me neither, but they seem like nice people."

"Yeah, I guess," said Odelia, but she didn't sound convinced.

Chase must have picked up on her inflection, for he said, "You know something I don't?"

"Oh, it's just that one of them is writing a book, apparently, detailing all the secrets she's learned about her friends over the years."

"She's doing what?"

"She's a recovering alcoholic herself—Michele Droba's sister-in-law Isobel. And she deeply feels that secrets are poisonous. They poison our minds and our relationships with others. Which is why she's been writing her autobiography."

"It's not her place to reveal other people's secrets, though, is it?"

"She seems to believe that it is. That she's doing her friends a favor."

"She's going to reveal Marge and Tex's secrets, too?"

"I guess so. Which is why Mom and Dad are worried."

"I didn't even know your mom and dad had secrets," said Chase as he took an onion from the larder and started chopping it into little pieces.

"Look at the way Chase is attacking that poor, defenseless onion," said Dooley.

"It's a vegetable, Dooley. It's not a living, breathing creature."

"Still. He's feeling the guilt. Just look at him crying."

"It'll be fine," said Chase. "How bad can those secrets be?" He gave his wife a curious look. "Do you know what your parents' secrets are?"

Odelia smiled as she directed another spoon into Grace's mouth. This time the food ended up in the right place, and not all over the little girl's bib. "I'm sure I don't, babe. And even if I did, what kind of daughter would I be if I told you?"

"I'm your husband, babe. You can tell me anything. I'm very discreet."

Odelia laughed. "I know. But they're not my secrets to tell, okay?"

"Okay," Chase agreed reluctantly, and attacked that poor

lonely onion with renewed fervor, throwing a couple of carrots into the mix just because he could.

Dooley looked on with a look of disapproval on his face. "Poor carrots," he murmured. "What have they ever done to you?"

CHAPTER 9

Marge was in bed, listening to her husband's slow, even breathing. It always amazed her how Tex could sleep so soundly, no matter the circumstances. She was one of those people who had a hard time going to sleep at night. She could lie awake for hours if something was going on in her life that worried her. Like now, with this whole business with Isobel's book. She'd already discussed things with Michele, who said there was nothing that she could do about it.

Their hostess seemed as annoyed about the prospect of their personal lives being laid bare as the rest of them, but Isobel was determined to go through with her 'process' as she called it. She didn't seem to care that she was dragging all of them along in her process, unwilling victims in one person's path to redemption.

She wondered what her husband's secret might be. Even though Tex said he had no secrets, there must be something, for a worried look had stolen over his face when Michele had told them about the book her sister-in-law was writing. If he didn't have secrets, why the worried look? She still wanted to believe him, though. After twenty-five years of marriage you'd think she knew this man. Knew everything about him. And yet. How well did you really know a person? Even couples who had been married for years still surprised each other. Things from their past suddenly came to light. Like secret second families or criminal offenses.

She didn't think Tex was a criminal, though. The thought was laughable. And she didn't think he had a second family in a different state either. A second wife, kids… Maybe this family had a dog instead of a pair of cats. And he wasn't a doctor, surely, but maybe an itinerant trader? She glanced down at her hubby, then dismissed the thought once more. How could he have a second family if he had to see his patients every day. He simply didn't have the opportunity.

But that her husband had a secret, of that she was certain. When she'd broached the subject he'd been dismissive first, then irritated, which was as much an admission of guilt as coming right out and saying what the big secret was.

She took her phone from the nightstand and checked the time. Ten to two. Christ. Wasn't she ever going to be able to sleep? She'd once read that if you couldn't sleep you shouldn't stay in bed but get up and read something—preferably something tedious. That way your brain got distracted from whatever was bothering you and soon got tired, allowing you to switch off. Maybe she should do that now. She'd brought along a couple of the latest bestsellers. Though she knew that if she started reading she'd still be going strong by the time daybreak came. And then she'd be so tired all day she wouldn't be able to enjoy their time together.

She turned once more, fluffed up her pillow and plunked her head down, willing sleep finally to come.

And that's when she heard it.

A scream—somewhere nearby.

Immediately she poked her husband in the ribs. "Tex! Wake up!"

"Mhwhatsthatwhat?" muttered the doctor, smacking his lips.

"Did you hear that?" she said, and kept perfectly still.

"Hear what?"

"Shh!"

She listened intently, but all was quiet once more. Almost as if the night had swallowed up the scream and smothered it under a thick blanket. Or maybe she hadn't heard a scream at all. Maybe it was all in her head. She had been thinking about a particularly successful horror novel she'd brought along to read.

"I don't hear anything," said Tex finally.

"I thought I heard a scream," she said.

"Must be those dogs the Ona woman brought. Even though it said clearly on the invitation 'No pets allowed.'" He turned over to his side. "There's always one who can't follow the rules, isn't there?" And he promptly went back to sleep.

For a few more minutes Marge lay listening, but no more screams were forthcoming. And finally her eyes drooped closed, and before long, she fell into a deep sleep, dreaming of strange screams in the night, and rabid dogs tearing the flesh from human bones.

※

If his wife thought Tex was enjoying a peaceful and unencumbered slumber, she was very much mistaken. While she was lying awake, so was he, only he didn't feel the need to tell her. It was true he had been asleep, even though it had taken a while, but when she had prodded him in the ribs, he'd been rudely brought out of that hard-won slumber, and once he had, he found it hard to go back to sleep.

And so he lay awake, his arms supporting his head, while he watched his wife sleep. He should never have told Isobel. Then she wouldn't have been able to put the things he told her in that stupid book of hers. But the woman was so easy to talk to. Maybe it was because of the things she'd gone through, but she had this way of putting you at ease, and extracting confidences from a person. He had always enjoyed talking to her. She was an attractive woman, of course. And in some ways a tragic person. After her husband had killed his brother, in circumstances that still weren't completely clear to him, he'd fled the country, leaving his wife and daughter to fend for themselves in a hostile world.

Isobel had briefly been arrested, but released as soon as the authorities had been satisfied that she had nothing whatsoever to do with the dreadful business. Alison Droba was fourteen when her father disappeared from their lives, and Isobel had been forced to stay strong for her daughter's sake, raising her as a single mother. Secretly she'd been driven to drink, hiding the habit from her daughter. A functioning alcoholic, in other words. Until Alison had gone off to college, and had turned her mom into an empty nester. This was when she'd thrown off the last inhibitions and had descended into a hell of her own making.

The story was well-known amongst her friends and family. One weekend things had come to a head, when Alison had come home from college, finding her mom incoherent and rambling at the foot of the stairs, and called an ambulance. The indignation pushed Isobel to find help, first with a hospital chaplain, who steered her in the direction of her local AA chapter, and somehow she found the strength to kick the habit, for her daughter's sake, but also for the sake of her own sanity.

And now she was writing that book. Part of her process. Part of the twelve-step program, she claimed, even though it said nowhere in any twelve-step program Tex had ever heard about that you had to rat out your friends to find salvation. It was probably that stupid chaplain's idea. He must have planted this idea into Isobel's head. If he could just get his hands on the guy…

He wondered now what Marge's secret could be. That she had a secret, that much was obvious from her reaction to the news Isobel was writing that infernal book. But no matter how much he pressed her to reveal her secret to him, she wouldn't. What could it be? A secret affair? A love child with another man? He'd read enough Harlan Coben novels for his imagination to run wild. Maybe her name wasn't even Marge Lip. And maybe Vesta wasn't her mother, nor Alec her brother. Maybe she was the secret love child of a politician? Or some mobster?

Or maybe in a previous life she'd killed someone, and now she had to live with the guilt. Maybe she was one of those killer kids, who'd murdered a man when she was eleven, and had been given a new identity, so that she could start a new life. And once her secret was out, a revenge mob would come after her. Which meant they'd come after him, too. Which meant their lives were over.

God. How he wished they'd never crossed paths with Isobel Droba.

CHAPTER 10

When Marge opened her eyes, light was already seeping into the room. Tex was still fast asleep, but when she stirred, he stirred, too. He glanced up at her with a smile. "Hey, beautiful. Sleep well?"

"Terrible," she said with a sigh.

"Same here. Must be the lack of cats."

She had to smile at that. "I never thought I'd hear you say that."

"I never thought I'd feel that way about those furballs. But I'm starting to think that their presence helps us sleep, don't you?"

"It's possible," she said. It was true that cats have a relaxing influence, though Tex had always complained about them hogging space at the foot of the bed, and causing him to have to tuck in his legs. Marge, because she was shorter than him, didn't have that particular problem.

"I always thought I'd be able to sleep so much better without the cats, but now I can see I was wrong," said Tex, and stretched and yawned. "Did I dream this, or did you wake me up last night because you heard a scream?"

"I did hear a scream," Marge confirmed. "At least I thought I did."

"Could be your overactive imagination."

"Could be," she agreed. It was a conclusion she'd reached herself already.

"Who are we playing today?" asked Tex as he reluctantly threw back the covers.

"I'm playing Michele and you're playing Max Stinger."

"Ooh, the plastic surgeon. Nice."

"Don't bore him too much with shoptalk, honey. You're here to play tennis, not stage a medical conference."

"I won't, I promise," said Tex. "Unless he begins first, of course." He gave her a kiss on the cheek, which led to a cuddle, which led to more kisses in other places.

Marge smiled up at her hubby. "You don't happen to have a secret family tucked away somewhere in Idaho, do you?"

Tex barked a surprised laugh. "What?"

"Never mind. Do you want to hit the shower first, or shall I?"

But before they could decide on the bathroom business, suddenly a loud scream echoed through the hallway. And this time it was not her imagination, for Tex had heard it, too.

It was a loud, drawn-out scream, then morphed into a series of short staccato bursts. Whoever it was, it sounded like something terrible had happened.

They both hurried out of the bed and into the corridor. They weren't the only ones, either, for doors were opening everywhere, and guests were streaming into the hallway, drawn to the agonized sounds of a woman desperately sobbing.

"It's coming from Isobel's room!" Tex said.

And as they all descended on the room, Perlita Gruner came stumbling out. The woman's face was white as a sheet, and obviously it was she who'd been screaming, for she uttered one now as she bumped into her husband.

"She's dead!" Perlita cried as her husband wrapped her in his arms. "Oh, my God, Nate, I think she's dead!"

Tex was the first to move past the couple and into the room, the determined look of a professional on his face. Marge was a close second, for she now wondered if that scream she'd heard last night could be connected to what Perlita had seen in that room?

And as she walked in, immediately she halted. For a moment, she didn't understand what she was seeing. For there, spread out across the carpet, Isobel Droba was lying in a pool of blood. Her chest was covered in blood, too, and so was her head. Her eyes were open and vacantly staring into space.

Tex knelt down next to the woman and felt for a pulse. But it was obvious that she was dead. His curt shake of the head confirmed this.

"Best if we don't touch anything," said Marge. She glanced around, her eyes immediately drawn to the window for some reason. Glass was on the floor, the window broken and open, a cold draft lowering the temperature in the room.

"We better call your brother," said Tex as they retreated to the door.

Marge closed the door, careful to use the sleeve of her pajamas as she did. To the crowd that had gathered outside, she said, "I'm afraid something happened to Isobel and it's important we don't enter the room or disturb the scene."

"Scene? You mean crime scene?" asked Max Stinger. The plastic surgeon was amongst the only ones dressed already, the others all donning dressing gowns.

"I'm afraid so," said Marge.

Michele was staring at her, wide-eyed. "You mean Isobel is…"

"Dead," Tex confirmed.

"Oh, my God!" Ona cried, hugging herself. "This isn't happening!"

"Let's all try to stay calm," Marge suggested. "And until the police arrive, no one leaves the house. They'll want to talk to all of us."

"How did she die?" asked Max Stinger, a look of concern on his face. He was directing his question to Tex, one medical professional to another.

"I'm not sure, actually," said Tex, bringing a hand to his white mane.

"There's a lot of blood," said Perlita in a quaky voice. Her hands were shaking, Marge saw, and her eyes were red-rimmed and teary. "There's blood everywhere!"

A murmur of surprise raced through the small group. "You mean she was—she was killed?!" Ona cried, her voice rising a full octave.

Perlita nodded. "So much blood," she repeated tremulously.

"That means the killer could still be in the house!" said Ona.

"There's a broken window," Marge said. "Maybe... a burglar?"

"I'm not staying in a house with a killer!" Ona said, starting to remove herself from the group. "I'm leaving! And I would advise all of you to do the same!"

"You're not going anywhere!" a clear voice rang out. They all looked up. It was the voice of Vena Aleman, and it brooked no contest. "We're all staying right here until the police decide otherwise. And that means you, too, Ona."

"But..."

"No buts. A murder has been committed, and the police are going to want to question each and every one of us. So we're all staying put. Is that understood?"

Nods of acquiescence all around. When the veterinarian spoke, everyone listened, whether they be pets or pet parents or in fact anyone. Vena had that presence and that authority. In another life she could have been a cop, Marge thought, as she gave Vena a grateful nod, which the vet returned in kind. A stampede for the exit was the last thing they wanted.

And so she picked up her phone, and called her brother.

CHAPTER 11

I was asleep at the foot of the bed when the sound of insistent ringing brought me out of my peaceful slumber. "The doorbell, Max," said Dooley sleepily.

I wasn't sure what he meant by that. It's hardly a big secret that cats are not in the capacity to open doors. We rely on our humans for such menial tasks. In this instance, however, both humans were conked out on the bed, after they'd gone to bed at a late hour, owing to some TV show they'd insisted on binge-watching. I could have told them this was a bad idea, but apparently the show was so good they didn't care whether such a late-night session would leave them tired and grumpy the next morning. Instant gratification, I think this is often called.

The fact that Grace had become a more regular sleeper lately, and didn't wake us all up at all hours of the night, might have had something to do with this. The little girl now went to bed at an early hour, and mostly slept through the night. And so her folks had started taking advantage of the fact by staying up late.

"Nothing that a good cup of coffee won't fix," Odelia had

told me when I'd made careful murmurings about persisting with this reckless folly.

I don't mind watching television, of course, but this habit of watching hours and hours of the same show frankly strikes me as a complete waste of valuable time. There are so many other things one can do. Such as there are: bird-watching—one of my favorite pastimes and something I like to devote great chunks of my own time to—or listening to the sounds of a minor critter trying to dig a hole through the outer wall of our home. Or even watching a spider crawl up the living room wall—sometimes they need several attempts to get all the way up there.

"Is that your phone?" Chase finally murmured.

"No, I think it's yours," Odelia returned halfheartedly.

For a moment all was quiet, then the ringing started up again.

From her own little bed, Grace made quiet murmurings, but slept on.

"Max, the doorbell," Dooley repeated, as if I was a Downton Abbey butler.

"I know it's the doorbell," I said. "But what do you want me to do about it?"

My friend opened his eyes and seemed to see me for the first time. "What?"

"The doorbell? You know as well as I do that cats don't open doors, Dooley."

"What are you talking about?"

It became clear to me now he'd been talking in his sleep, a habit he gets sometimes. "It's fine, Dooley. Don't worry about it," I said.

"Your phone, Chase," Odelia said plaintively.

"Your phone, babe," Chase returned, just as plaintively.

"Oh, for crying out loud!" I suddenly burst out. "It's the door!"

"What are you talking about?" said Odelia with a tired groan.

"There's someone at the door!"

"Oh, all right, hold your horses," she said, making a valiant attempt to open her eyes. She slipped one leg from underneath the covers, and before I knew what was happening, there was a sort of thud and Odelia was on the floor. "Oops," she said, then scrambled into a more or less upright position and headed for the door.

"I think she's sleepwalking, Max," said Dooley. "Look at her. She's still asleep."

He was right. Odelia was walking, but her eyes were firmly shut.

"Open your eyes, woman!" I cried, afraid she'd tumble down the stairs and break that delicate human neck of hers.

"Yes, sir," Odelia mumbled.

"It's not my phone," Chase said as he made an attempt to grab the device from the nightstand. "So it must be yours." The phone slipped from his nerveless grasp and hit the floor. "Darn it," the cop muttered, as his arm just dangled there.

"Are they on drugs, you think, Max?" asked Dooley, as he watched the sad spectacle. "They must be on drugs, acting so weird."

"Yes, they are," I said with a frown. "The drug of binge-watching."

Downstairs things seemed to be happening, for I could hear the door being opened and moments later the nervous tones of Uncle Alec's voice reached my ears.

"There's been a murder," the police chief was saying. "At your mom and dad's tennis retreat."

These words finally shook Odelia into full wakefulness, for I could hear her say, "What?!"

"Your folks are fine. It's one of the hosts that's been murdered. Some woman named Isobel Droba?"

"Oh, my God."

"Yeah. Where's Chase? Can you guys get over there pronto?"

"Chase!" Odelia bellowed. "Babe, get down here!"

"All right, all right," the cop said. "Where's the fire?"

"There's been a murder!" Uncle Alec shouted at the foot of the stairs.

This statement had the desired effect on the stalwart police detective. He jerked into an upright position, and moments later was thundering down the stairs. If his superior officer took offense by the casual wear his underling had donned—naked torso and floral-patterned boxers—he didn't show it. Instead he proceeded to fill the detective in on some of the details of the case, then entrusted it into his capable hands.

"Looks like it's time to get up," said Dooley with a muscular yawn.

"Yeah, looks that way," I agreed, and since yawns are infectious, I went through one myself.

And so it was that while our humans halved their usual bathroom time and kitchen time, Dooley and myself patiently waited until they were ready to move out. They still didn't look entirely chipper and ready for duty, but then humans rarely do when they're being dragged out of bed at some ungodly hour.

After placing Grace in the capable care of Gran, instructing her to drop the toddler off at the daycare center at her earliest convenience, we were off.

We arrived at the house Michele Droba had rented—an Airbnb, apparently—posthaste, and judging from the police vehicles parked haphazardly in the drive, and the coroner's van, the investigation was already underway, even though the actual detective being assigned to the case hadn't yet arrived. But then I guess that's often the way: the star of the show is frequently the last one to arrive.

The villa was a large one, as villas go, and located on the outskirts of Hampton Cove, that fair and friendly town in the Hamptons. It was a large place, with a nice paved forecourt and plenty of well-manicured greenery all around.

"It doesn't look like an Airbnb, Max," said Dooley as we got out of Chase's squad car. "It looks more like one of those posh mansions celebrities occupy."

It did look like a posh celebrity dwelling. And that's probably because there were several celebrities staying at the place. Or at least such were the rumors. And so as we entered, I wondered if we'd run into Beyoncé, or Tom Cruise, or even that skinny guy from those Spider-man movies. Unfortunately for us no celebrities were actually present, as soon became clear when we were led up the stairs by one of the officers on the scene, who gave us a list of the guests.

Michele Droba was the person organizing the tennis extravaganza, and the woman who'd been found dead was her sister-in-law Isobel Droba. Michele's boyfriend Christopher Bonarowski was a publisher of some renown but not famous enough to register on my personal radar. Then there were Marge and Tex, of course. And also Vena Aleman—a person with whom Dooley and I were intimately familiar, to our eternal regret, since she's a veterinarian. In spite of adhering to some of the strictures of the Nazi Party, Vena had managed to ensnare a husband, a man named Glenn for some reason.

Also present in the house at this time were a Perlita and Nathan Gruner, who were something important in the art world according to the police officer. And Ona Konpacka and boyfriend.

"Ona Konpacka!" Dooley cried excitedly. "But we know Ona, don't we, Max!"

"We most certainly do," I said, well pleased by this surprise.

We'd met Ona on a previous case, where she was a suspect. She was a former supermodel, whose exceedingly good looks had been marred to some extent by a hack plastic surgeon, and I wondered how she'd fared since our last meeting.

We had arrived upstairs and were led into the room where the unfortunate victim had been found that morning. Isobel Droba was lying on the floor, partially obscured by the large bulk of the county medical examiner Abe Cornwall. The frizzy-haired medical professional was frowning as he studied the body, his electric hair standing on end as if he'd just stuck his fingers in a wall socket.

"So what's the verdict, Abe?" asked Chase as he donned plastic gloves and booties.

"She's dead," said Abe curtly.

"I thought as much. What made her so?"

"Blow to the back of the head, most likely."

"Most likely?" asked Chase, directing a glance to the window, which was broken.

"She's also been stabbed, so it's a toss-up. Could be the blunt-force trauma that killed her, or the stab wounds. I'll know more once I get her on my slab."

"Stabbed with a knife, was she?"

"I'm not sure," said the coroner, looking distinctly unhappy. It was hard to say whether this was because of the early hour, or because the killer was making things difficult for him. "Some sharp object, at any rate." He got up with a groan. "And before you ask, she was killed sometime during the night. I'd say between seven and five hours ago."

Chase checked his phone. "That would put time of death between one and three."

Abe didn't deign him with a reply. "Did you know your mom and dad are here?" He was directing his question at Odelia, his face screwed up in curiosity.

"Yeah, I know," said Odelia as she studied the body. "Tennis retreat," she explained. "They have one of these every year. Same circle of friends."

"Nice work if you can get it," said Abe vaguely.

"Could be a break-in," said Chase, pointing to the broken window.

"We better check if anything was stolen," said Odelia. "Who found the body?"

The officer who'd been the first to arrive on the scene consulted his notebook. "A Mrs. Perlita Gruner. She and her husband Nathan are in the next room."

Odelia nodded her appreciation. "Anything missing?"

"I'm not sure," said the officer. "There's no phone, no laptop, no wallet as far as I can tell. But whether they've gone missing…"

The inference was obvious: Odelia would have to find out herself if she wanted to know the answer to this question.

"Oh, and your mom wants to talk to you," said the officer. "She was in the next room—the one over there," he explained, looking a little sheepish. It isn't often that relatives of the detecting duo were in the house where a murder took place.

"Looks like Marge and Tex are suspects," I told Dooley as I glanced around the room.

"Suspects!" Dooley cried. "But why?! They're not murderers!"

"You never know, Dooley," I said. "Anyone can be a murderer."

"But not Marge or Tex!"

I traipsed around the room, feeling the eyes of Abe's team of crime scene technicians poking holes in my back. Nobody likes people trampling all over their crime scene, and pets even less—shedding hair where no hair should be. But I wanted to get a good overview of the scene. The poor woman had been killed in what looked like a pretty frenzied attack, and already I could tell that this murder business spelled trouble with a capital T for Odelia's parents.

"There's a drainpipe," said the officer helpfully, pointing to the window. "So the killer could easily have climbed it and gained entrance that way."

Odelia and Chase checked the veracity of this statement, and finally Chase nodded his agreement. "Must be the way they came in," he agreed, then turned on his heel. "I'll go and check for footprints."

"And don't forget about cigarette butts!" Dooley cried at the detective's retreating back. He turned to me. "Footprints and cigarette butts. Very important clues."

"Even more important is the murder weapon," I said. "Or murder weapons, plural."

"They haven't been found?"

"No, Dooley, they have not."

CHAPTER 12

We met Marge in the hallway, or at least Odelia met her, and we tagged along. For the benefit of privacy we used the bedroom Marge and Tex were staying in for the duration of the retreat.

"So you're saying you heard a scream?" asked Odelia.

Marge nodded. She looked stricken, which wasn't surprising since she'd just stumbled across the dead body of a friend. "Around two o'clock. I thought it must have been a dream, but now I'm not so sure."

"I didn't hear anything," said Tex decidedly.

"You were sleeping," said Marge, as if accusing her husband of a grave offense. "While I was lying awake all night."

Tex opened his mouth to speak, but then seemed to think better of it and closed it again.

"You couldn't sleep because of the scream?" asked Odelia.

"Oh, no. You could say that was the cherry on the cake, so to speak." She hesitated, then said, "Isobel was writing a book. A book she says she was filling with secrets of all the people she knew. So naturally we've all been on tenterhooks wondering what she's going to write about us."

"You don't have any secrets, though, right?"

"Oh, no, of course not. And neither does Tex. But still." She chewed her bottom lip nervously. "Isobel was a recovering alcoholic, and coming clean was part of her process." She shrugged. "I guess we were all unsure what she was going to write. Whether true or false, it might be damaging to the reputation of the people present."

"Very damaging," Tex muttered darkly. As a doctor, he was a public figure, and had his reputation to think about, same as anyone in his position. So I could imagine he wasn't happy about this tell-all book Isobel Droba had been in the process of penning.

"Do you think this murder could be connected to the book?" asked Odelia the obvious question.

"I thought it was a break-in?" asked Tex, looking up sharply.

"We're not sure exactly what happened," Odelia explained. "Though it certainly looks as if her room was broken into last night."

"There's something else you must know," said Marge tentatively.

"Yes?" Odelia encouraged her.

"Yesterday, when we got back from our doubles game, I heard a fight in Isobel's room. Isobel and her daughter Alison. Something about Alison wanting to marry this man she's been seeing. Jason Rocamora. Jason is an ex-con, apparently, and Isobel wanted her daughter to break it off with him. Instead, Alison said she wanted to marry him, and Isobel wasn't happy about that. She threatened to cut Alison off financially."

Odelia was scribbling all this down on her tablet, nodding all the while. "She was rich, was she, Isobel?"

"I guess so," said Marge. She emitted a curt laugh. "It's not a topic that's come up in conversation, but I've always assumed she and Michele are well-off."

"That would be Michele Droba, her… sister-in-law?"

"Yes. Michele married Dean Droba and Isobel married Dean's brother Gavin."

Odelia looked up. "I thought Michele was staying here with a man named Chris…" She consulted her notes. "Christopher Bonarowski. A publisher?"

Marge nodded, crossing her arms in front of her chest. "Dean died. It's a terrible story. He and his brother got into some kind of argument one night and Gavin gave his brother a shove. Dean fell and hit his head against something sharp— I think the edge of a desk or a chair if I remember correctly —and he died. Consequently Gavin fled the country and hasn't been seen since."

"So Michele is a widow and Isobel's husband went missing?"

"It's not a story a lot of people are familiar with. But since Tex and I have been friends with Michele for so long…"

"Michele doesn't talk about her husband," said Tex. "And neither did Isobel."

"I can understand why," said Odelia. "When was this?"

"Oh, must be almost ten years ago now."

"Seven," Marge corrected her husband.

"Seven," Tex echoed, cutting his wife a curious look.

"Okay, and you were both in this room when Isobel was killed?" asked Odelia. When her parents looked at her, clearly aghast, she shrugged. "I have to ask."

"Of course," said Marge. "As I said I was having trouble sleeping, so I was awake the first part of the night. But I never left the room, and neither did your dad."

"I also had trouble sleeping, actually," Tex muttered. "Must be the bed."

"Yeah, that must be it," said Marge, though she didn't look convinced.

I was wondering what else was going on here. For some reason the couple was acting a little evasive. As if they were hiding something. Hard to drag them over the coals and extract a full confession, though, being that they were Odelia's mom and dad and all.

"Okay, so is there anything else you can think of? Anything out of the ordinary?"

"Like what?" asked Tex, who was tiring of the barrage of questions.

"Like… how did Isobel strike you? Same as usual? Different?"

"She seemed tense," said Marge. "At first I figured it had something to do with this book she was writing. But then yesterday I thought it must be connected with Alison and her affair with her ex-criminal."

"That must have weighed on her mind," Odelia agreed. "Anything else? Dad?"

But Tex shook his head. "Nothing I can think of. We were having a nice time here, all of us, so this murder business came out of the blue. Must be a burglary gone wrong," he added his opinion.

"Was anything stolen from your room?"

Tex glanced around, as if the question hadn't occurred to him, and frowned. "I don't think so," he said. "My phone is still here, my wallet… Your purse, honey?"

"Purse is here," Marge confirmed. "And so is my phone. Nothing stolen, I think."

"Good," said Odelia as she tapped her tablet. "And how are you holding up?" Her voice was tinged with a note of concern. She had put her detective cap off and was donning the worried daughter cap now.

"It was a big shock," Marge confessed.

"You knew Isobel well, of course."

"We did," said Tex. "Have known her for years."

When nothing more seemed forthcoming, the parents still continuing to be strangely reticent, we took our leave, after Odelia had issued her usual warning not to leave the premises, and if anything came to mind, to tell her immediately.

"I had the feeling they were hiding something," I told Odelia the moment we left the room.

"I had the same impression," our human confirmed. "But what?"

"You don't think they murdered Isobel, do you?" Dooley asked, shocked.

"No, I don't think they killed Isobel. But they're lying about something."

CHAPTER 13

When Chase had returned from his excursions, he regrettably informed us that he hadn't found any suspicious footprints below Isobel Droba's window, owing to the fact that the drainpipe didn't end in a nice flower bed, as it often does in an Agatha Christie novel, but on the paved forecourt, which isn't as susceptible to footprints as loose sand.

"And what about cigarette butts?" asked Dooley, who seemed to have developed a keen interest in this staple of many a Sherlock Holmes story.

"No cigarette butts either," Odelia informed us with a twinkle in her eye.

"That's too bad," said Dooley. "I definitely thought there would be butts."

"No butts," I said, and then it was time to enter into our investigation proper by talking to Michele Droba, the victim's sister-in-law.

Michele met us in one of the downstairs rooms, this one a modestly appointed living room where cream-colored leather couches awaited us, as well as a smattering of modern art paintings adorning the walls.

"Perlita Gruner's work," Michele explained when she saw Chase checking out a painting of a green apple on a red background. "She owns an art gallery in town."

"Just to be sure: this isn't your home, is it?" asked Chase.

"Oh, no. It belongs to a friend of mine. Cyril Baskerville. He rents it out as an Airbnb. It's perfect for us, since it has two tennis courts out back as well as a swimming pool. In fact we've been using it for just about forever—long before Airbnb even existed. Back then Cyril rented out the place through a real estate agency owned by his brother. When his brother retired he switched to Airbnb."

"But you're still here," said Odelia with a smile, which Michele returned.

We all took a seat, and Chase launched into the interview. "First off, my sincerest condolences, Mrs. Droba. Isobel's death must come as a great shock to you."

"It does," Michele confirmed. "Isobel and I were very close, and losing her is like losing a sister."

"You weren't actually sisters, though, were you?"

"No. Isobel was married to my husband's brother."

"Did you have a chance to see if anything was taken from her room?" asked Odelia.

"I did, yes, and as far as I can tell her laptop is gone, and so is her phone and her wallet. Looks like the person who broke in and killed her took everything."

"The odd thing is that this burglar, this thief, didn't target anyone else."

"He probably wasn't expecting to be caught," said Michele. "And so when Isobel wasn't in bed as he'd surmised, and caught him red-handed going through her things, he must have killed her and escaped the same way he came in."

Chase nodded thoughtfully. "Have you had problems with break-ins before?"

"No, never."

"And there's no alarm system? No CCTV cameras on the property?"

"There is an alarm system, but we don't arm it unless we leave the house. And now during this week it's never armed, since there's always someone here."

"And what about cameras?"

"No cameras, I'm afraid. Cyril believes they might scare off potential guests." She smiled. "Not everyone likes to be filmed, Detective. Or their every movement clocked by some unknown security person miles away who can do who knows what with the footage. Put it on YouTube, perhaps, or turn it into a TikTok video."

"I see," said Chase. "So we have no way of knowing who this mystery burglar-slash-killer was."

"Oh, I have a pretty good idea," said Michele, surprising us all. "My niece Alison is involved with a man named Jason Rocamora. Mr. Rocamora is a violent criminal and has spent time in prison for various crimes. In fact Isobel had engaged a private detective agency to keep tabs on the man, and make sure he didn't harm Alison. And also, Isobel told me just yesterday that Alison planned to marry this criminal, and that she told her daughter that if she was going through with the wedding, she would cut her off financially. I guess Mr. Rocamora didn't like that."

"You think he's the one who broke in last night?"

Michele nodded soberly. "You have to know that Isobel was working on a book. Her autobiography. She was under contract with a publisher, who'd offered her a sizable advance on royalties. As far as I know the manuscript was on her laptop. So whoever took that laptop now has the only copy of Isobel's book." She raised a meaningful eyebrow. "My boyfriend is Isobel's publisher, so I know how much she was paid for the book. And now that Jason has the laptop, I'm sure he'll be in touch soon, demanding money in exchange for the manuscript."

"How did this Jason Rocamora know about the book?" asked Odelia.

"Alison will have told him. She knew what her mother was writing."

"How much did your boyfriend pay for the book?" asked Chase.

"One million dollars," said Michele, watching Chase closely.

The cop didn't disappoint. He whistled through his teeth.

"Why so much?" asked Odelia. "Isobel wasn't famous, was she?"

"No, she wasn't. But she knew a lot of famous people, and she was promising to write a tell-all book, no holds barred. She didn't believe in secrets, you see, and said she wanted to expose them in her book." When Chase and Odelia eyed her curiously, she added, "I probably should have prefaced that by saying that my husband and Isobel's husband ran the Droba Group for a while, which is one of the biggest tire companies in the world. The company was founded over a hundred years ago by one of Dean and Gavin's forebears. It was run by my father-in-law Bill, who relinquished the reins to his sons. But when Dean died and Gavin disappeared, Bill took over again, and is still running the company today."

"So it's safe to say that Isobel knew a lot of very important people," said Chase, summing things up nicely.

"And a lot of those very important people are going to be in her book—all of their so-called secrets exposed. Which is why she was paid the one million."

"For a gossip book?"

"Everybody likes gossip, Detective Kingsley. Especially about the rich and famous."

"Do you know the name of the detective agency Isobel contacted?" asked Odelia.

"Of course. And I'm sure they'll be able to tell you what Jason Rocamora is planning to do with Isobel's laptop. They promised to keep a close eye on him."

CHAPTER 14

While Chase did a quick check to see if this Rocamora character had a criminal record, Odelia talked to her dad again.

"Secrets? What secrets? I don't know anything about secrets," Tex blustered.

"Well, Isobel was writing a tell-all book about the people that have passed through her life," Odelia said. "So you guys must have discussed this during the past week, seeing as you've known each other for so long, right?"

"I don't know anything about any secrets," Tex insisted. "And anyway, why is this important? I thought Isobel was the victim of some burglar? Some thief?"

"This burglar might have been after the book," said Odelia. "Isobel's laptop was stolen, and Michele just told us that Isobel's manuscript is worth a great deal of money."

"I guess," said Tex, his eyes fixed on some point in the middle distance. This was obviously a man who wanted to be anywhere but here, and talking about anything but Isobel and her book.

"So to your recollection, nobody here mentioned that manuscript, Dad?"

Tex turned decidedly shifty-eyed. "No, nobody. Whatever was going on with that book, this is the first thing I'm hearing about it."

"Okay, fine," said Odelia, visibly disappointed in her dad. "How about Mom?"

"What about your mom?"

"She never mentioned the book?"

"No, she did not," said Tex.

Chase had returned, thoughtfully clutching his phone. "Michele was right. Jason Rocamora does have a criminal record. Aggravated robbery. Assault and battery. Sounds like a seriously wrong dude."

"Well, there you have it," said Tex with satisfaction. "Case closed. Now can we go about our business?"

"Mh? Oh, no, buddy," said Chase. "I'm afraid you can't leave the premises. At least not until Alec says you can."

"But you've got your guy!"

"Maybe."

"God," said the doctor, and stomped off, looking none too happy.

We all stared after him. "What's going on with your dad?" asked Chase.

"I'm not sure. He's acting really strange," said Odelia. "Him and Mom both."

"I've been trying to get a hold of the detective assigned to Jason Rocamora," said Chase, "and they've promised he'll phone me back as soon as he can."

"Let's hope we can wrap up this case as soon as possible. Keeping these people cooped up in here is going to prove a challenge. Are you sure we can't allow them to go home?"

"It's fine for Tex and Marge, but what about the others? Not all of them live in Hampton Cove. And if we allow one set of couples to go home and not the others, it's going to create trouble. No, as long as we haven't ruled out that someone on the premises killed Isobel Droba, we need to keep a close eye on these people."

When we entered the living room to talk to the next couple, imagine my surprise when a familiar cute little dog greeted us on the threshold. It looked like an Ewok, but in actual fact it was a miniature Brussels Griffon named Joey, and last time I looked belonged to Ona Konpacka, the former supermodel.

"Max! Dooley!" the little doggie exclaimed, clearly happy to see us.

"Joey!" said Dooley. "What are you doing here?"

"Ona doesn't go anywhere without me," said Joey.

"But I thought she was a recluse?" said Dooley.

"Oh, not anymore, she's not."

We glanced over to the window, where Ona was waiting for her police interview. And I have to say she looked a lot better than the last time we saw her. Back then her face was all lumpy. Now it was as smooth as a Swiss lake in wintertime. She was heavily made up, but still: the structure of her face had been restored to its former glory as far as I could tell.

"Who's that man next to her?" I asked.

"That's Max Stinger," said Joey. "He's the man who saved her life."

"Don't tell me Ona tried to take her own life!" Dooley cried.

Joey laughed. "Oh, no, nothing like that. But he performed the operation that made her look human again, repairing the damage that butcher caused."

With that butcher Joey was referring to the cosmetic

surgeon who had ended Ona's great career. "So he's her boyfriend now?" I asked.

"He is. I guess between the moment he put her under narcosis and the moment the bandages were removed and she was greeted by her old face again in the mirror, Ona fell in love. They've been together ever since."

A second little doggie came tripping up to us. "Who are these cats, Joey?" it asked. Like Joey, it was small and fluffy, and was clearly a Brussels Griffon, just like her.

"These are Max and Dooley," said Joey. "Remember I told you about them?"

"Oh, that's right. They're the ones who got me my new forever home."

"When you promised me you'd ask your human to tell Ona to get me a little brother or sister," said Joey, "I wasn't sure you'd keep your promise. So when Zoey suddenly showed up one day, I was pleasantly surprised." She looked a little bashful all of a sudden. "Thank you so much. You don't know what it meant to me."

"I think I do," I said. "Life at home wouldn't be the same for me without Dooley." Or Harriet and Brutus, of course. When we first met Joey, Ona had been living like a recluse in her apartment, with only Joey as her companion. The little doggie had been lonely, and had asked us to arrange for a friend to keep her company. And so we'd talked to Odelia, who'd told Marge, who knew that Michele had some vague connection to Ona, and thus things had been arranged.

"I'm happy to meet again," I said. "Even though the circumstances aren't great."

"No, a woman has been murdered, right?" said Joey. "Isobel Droba?"

"You didn't know Isobel well?"

"Not really. This is the first year we've been invited to this retreat. Last year Ona was still holed up in her apartment."

"It's nice here," said Zoey, with a touch of bashfulness. "People are all so very nice to us—and to Ona and Max."

"Max?" asked Dooley, then got the reference and laughed. "Oh, that's funny, Max. Ona's boyfriend is also called Max. Just like you!"

"I know," I said, even though I didn't get the joke. "You didn't hear anything last night?" I asked. "Or notice anything suspicious?"

"Nothing," said Joey. "It's all very new to us, of course. We don't know most of these people. The only person Ona knows is Michele, who once organized a photo shoot for some campaign about car tires." She smiled. "I remember Ona complaining that it's hard work to make a car tire look sexy. But she managed."

"Is she going to be a model again?" asked Dooley.

"No, she's retired. Her face is still not fully recovered. Maybe it never will. And besides, that part of her life is behind her now. She's happy that she can be out and about again. And it's all thanks to Max."

When Dooley stared at me, I said, "Not me, Dooley. The other Max."

"Oh, right," said my friend, then laughed again. "It's very confusing, Max. Maybe we should call you Max 1 and Ona's boyfriend Max 2. Or the other way around."

"I think we'll manage to differentiate between the two," I said dryly.

CHAPTER 15

Chase introduced Odelia as the civilian police consultant assisting him on the case, and at the mention of the name, Ona's hitherto regal and frosty demeanor melted to some extent. "You're Marge Poole's daughter, aren't you?" she said.

"Yep, that's me," Odelia confirmed.

"I can't thank you and your mom enough for telling Michele to get a friend for Joey," said the former model. "She's been so happy since I got Zoey."

"I know from experience how lonely our furry friends can be when they're the only pets we've got," said Odelia. She gestured to Dooley and me. "These two are never apart. They play together, sleep together, share their meals together." Sleuth together, I thought.

"Same here," said Ona. "I'm so lucky that Joey and Zoey get along so well. They're like twins now. They even look as if they could be from the same litter."

"They're adorable," said Odelia as she admired Ona's twin pride and joy.

Chase cleared his throat. Clearly he felt there were other,

more pressing matters to discuss than Odelia and Ona's respective pet pairs. "So Isobel Droba," he said. "How well did you know her?"

"Not that well," said Ona. "I knew Michele from a shoot I once did for her, but I'd never met her sister before she invited me to this tennis retreat."

"Sister-in-law," Chase corrected her.

"Oh, they weren't sisters? I thought they were."

"Did you hear anything last night, Ona?" asked Odelia. "Or you, sir?"

The plastic surgeon shook his head. "Not a thing, I'm afraid. Slept like a log."

"I didn't hear anything either," said Ona. "But then I take a sleeping pill before I go to bed." She gingerly touched her face. "I suffered through multiple operations in a short space of time, and the nerve endings in my face are still very sensitive."

"It won't be like that forever," the surgeon assured her.

Ona gave him a grateful look. "It's improved a lot already."

"And it will keep improving—just you wait and see."

"So Isobel was writing her autobiography," said Chase. "And she was planning to name names and reveal secrets about the people she knew."

"Yes?" said Ona.

"It's possible that this book is connected to what happened to her."

"I thought she was killed by a burglar?" asked Max Stinger.

"One of the theories we're investigating right now is that she was murdered because of the manuscript," Chase explained. "Whoever did this stole her laptop, and that manuscript was on that laptop."

"Coincidence, surely," said the face doctor. "They probably grabbed whatever valuable things they could find."

"I never heard about this autobiography until now," said Ona. "So you think that's why she was killed? Because someone wanted to get their hands on it?"

"It's a possibility," said Chase.

"A very remote one, surely," said the doctor.

"So you weren't concerned that you were going to be in Isobel's autobiography?"

"Oh, no," said Ona with a smile. "I hardly knew the woman, and she hardly knew me. Besides, I have no secrets to hide, Detective. My life is an open book."

But as she said it, she lowered her lashes. A bad liar, I determined. Whatever Ona was hiding clearly had something to do with that fateful manuscript.

"How about you, sir?" asked Chase.

"What about me?" the surgeon said, frowning at the cop. "Secrets? I don't have any secrets. Nothing to hide. Just ask the IRS. Everything in order and above board!" And to emphasize how ridiculous Chase's suggestion was, he barked a hearty laugh.

I directed an inquisitive look at Joey and Zoey, who'd been following the interview with rapt attention. They had probably never been present at a police interview before, and were fascinated to watch it play out in real time, in front of their noses. "So what do you think, Joey?" I asked. "Could Ona or Max be involved in this murder business, you think?"

Joey's eyes went wide in shock. "Max, what are you saying! Of course not! Ona could never murder a person. Absolutely not. She's the sweetest person I know!"

"And how about her boyfriend?"

"Yeah, he's a surgeon," said Dooley. "And we all know that surgeons like to cut things open—people or pets. So is it possible he was suffering through acute withdrawal and found a perfect specimen in Isobel to practice his skills on?"

I wouldn't exactly have put it that way, but it did seem to me that a surgeon would know how to go about killing a person. Though what his exact motive would be was beyond me at that point.

"Max is a decent man," said Joey. "He would never harm anyone."

"He's a saint," Zoey chimed in. "A saint who saved Ona's life."

"He did save Ona's life. Because that's what he does."

"Doctors save lives, Max. They don't take it."

"Fine," I said, holding up my paw. "I get it. Ona wouldn't hurt a soul and Stinger is a saint. Still, saints can sin when pushed to the limit, and so can nice people like Ona. Especially when someone is threatening to expose their biggest secrets."

"Absolutely not," said Joey. "Ona doesn't have secrets, and neither has Max."

"This Max or that Max?" asked Dooley, just to make sure.

"I don't know about this Max," said Joey. "Maybe this Max does have secrets."

"No, he doesn't," I assured the little doggie with the funny face.

"Well, that Max doesn't have secrets either," said Joey with conviction.

"He's a saint," Zoey repeated. "And saints don't have secrets, Max."

It was obvious we had reached a dead end. And maybe they were right. Maybe Ona and Max Stinger had nothing to hide, and had nothing to do with what happened to Isobel. But I still had the impression that Ona hadn't answered truthfully when Chase put it to her that she might feature in Isobel's book.

CHAPTER 16

Chase had gone off to take another call, and in the meantime Odelia had decided to talk to her mom and dad some more. It so rarely happened that she had family members who'd been present in a house where a murder had taken place. And Marge had actually heard the woman scream. So maybe there was some detail, however small, the parent pair hadn't yet divulged to their detective daughter.

Dooley and I had other qualms: it was now going on eleven o'clock, and since no meals seemed forthcoming, and Odelia had neglected to pack us a lunch, we were left to our own devices when it came to rustling up something to tide us over until dinnertime rolled around.

"In a house this big, and filled with dogs, there has to be something to eat," Dooley said as we wended our way to the kitchen.

"It's only two dogs, though," I said. "And maybe Ona feeds them from her own little stock of dog food."

"Dog food, cat food, I don't care what we find. I'm not picky, Max."

I would have reminded him that he was a vegetarian now, but that seemed unduly harsh. So instead I said, "We're bound to find something to eat."

But the kitchen was eerily devoid of foodstuffs. No chef whipping something up and prepared to throw two hungry kitties a tasty morsel of something yummy. And no house guests enjoying an early lunch or late breakfast either. In fact the place looked deserted, with all the tasty stuff locked up inside gleaming cupboards and sizable fridges.

"Maybe they've hidden the stuff somewhere else?" Dooley suggested.

But before we could retreat, we heard footsteps coming hither, and hope once more surged in our bosoms—and our empty stomachs.

The footsteps belonged to Michele Droba, always a likely candidate to dispense with some of the good stuff, quickly followed by Ona Konpacka.

"Here should be fine," said Michele. "It's just us and those two kitties."

Ona eyed us with a touch of suspicion, but we returned her gaze with a look of absolute innocence—and expectation.

"So what was it you wanted to ask?" said Michele as she took a seat at the kitchen counter.

"It's the police. They've been asking me about Isobel's book. Wanting to know if I'm in it."

"Yeah, they seem to have taken a keen interest in Isobel's scribblings," Michele confirmed. "And for good reason, too."

"So that book is connected to her murder?"

"Of course it is. The man who took it probably wants to sell it to the highest bidder."

"Oh, God," Ona said as she touched her face, patting it gently as if she couldn't believe it was back in working order. "Tell me she didn't mention me in her book?"

"I wouldn't know, my dear. I haven't had the pleasure of reading it."

"But Chris. He's Isobel's publisher. So he must know."

"He doesn't. Isobel hadn't delivered him the manuscript yet."

"So Chris hasn't read it? Nobody has read it?"

"Nobody has read it," Michele assured the woman. "May I ask why you're so concerned about Isobel's book?"

Ona hesitated, but then the urge to confide in someone was stronger than her desire to keep it a secret. "She was easy to talk to, Isobel was."

"I know she was."

"I should never have told her."

Michele waited patiently while Ona was still struggling with her conflicting impulses. Finally, she said, "It happened a long time ago. At the beginning of my career. Or before, actually, back when I didn't have a career yet. I did have a sister, Katey. One year older than me. Beautiful, smart, and ambitious. She dreamed of being a model, and so did I. But my sister was pretty, and I was gangly as a teenager. Not pretty at all. And I wore glasses. So I knew I'd never be a model. And then one day a scout for one of the big modeling agencies spotted my sister at our local mall—we were living in Wisconsin back then. He asked her name and phone number, and said he'd be in touch." She took a deep breath. "Only when he did get in touch, I intercepted the message and went to the meeting instead. I deleted the message and never mentioned it to my sister. I got my hair done, ditched the glasses, went for a complete makeover. And I bagged a contract. The model scout was surprised to see me, but I explained that my sister had no interest in being a model but I did. So he took a chance on me."

Michele studied the former model. "And this is what you told Isobel? What you think might be in her book?"

Ona, who had taken a tissue and was dabbing at her eyes, nodded. "My sister doesn't know. Nobody does. And why I ever decided to tell Isobel, God only knows."

Michele grimaced. "She had a knack. People told her their deepest, darkest secrets and they didn't even know why. She was just that kind of person. Warm and kind, you know. She could look at you and you just knew you could trust her."

"Until she decided to write that stupid book," Ona said with vehemence.

"It's fine," said Michele, rubbing the woman's back. "I'm sure your story didn't even make Isobel's book. I'm sure she'll focus on her own life and her own secrets mostly. All this business about revealing other people's secrets was just her way of saying that we shouldn't live with this stuff. It just serves to drag us down."

"You think?"

"Absolutely."

"It's just that… I don't want anyone to know, especially my sister. But also Max. So if Chris gets his hands on that manuscript, could you… could he…" Her voice had taken on a beseeching quality.

"You want him to remove any passages referring to you and your sister?"

Ona nodded fervently. "Please. It's my story. I should be the one telling it—not some stranger I only met once, and in a moment of weakness confided in."

"I'll bet alcohol was involved?"

Ona smiled weakly. "Yes."

"I've often wondered why it's so much easier to confide in a stranger than it is in our nearest and dearest," Michele mused.

"Maybe it's exactly because they're strangers? No strings? You see them now, and you know you'll never see them again? If you tell your family, whatever you tell them will be like this thing that stands between you and ruins family dinners."

"I guess," said Michele. "I once told a stranger I met on a train things about myself I've never even told my husband or my parents. Like you said, I just figured I'd never see him again—and I never did."

"Well, aren't I the stupid one. I knew I'd see Isobel again and still I told her."

"Don't beat yourself up about it, Ona. Like I said, Isobel had that effect on people. It was her secret weapon. It's what we all liked about her." Then, more quietly, she added, "And perhaps it was also what got her killed."

CHAPTER 17

Okay, so now we knew all about Ona's secret, but we were still nowhere close to satisfying our appetite for something different than secrets and lies: real food!

Lucky for us, at that moment Joey and Zoey entered the kitchen, in search of their human. Joey took one look at us and said, "Are you guys hungry?"

We both nodded determinedly and the little doggie smiled.

"Come with us," she said. "We've got more food than we can handle."

That sounded like music to our ears, and so we quickly followed the Brussels Griffon pair out of the kitchen, up the stairs, and into the room Ona had claimed for her own. Joey led us straight to the window, where a veritable smorgasbord of food stood on display!

"Oh, my God!" said Dooley. "You guys!"

"Dig in," said Joey with a grin. "And don't worry about overdoing things. There's plenty more where this came from."

"It's dog food, though," said Zoey, issuing a health warning. "It might not contain the necessary proteins, vitamins and minerals you guys need."

"I don't care," I said with my mouth full of delicious nuggets. "It's food!"

"Max likes to get the first kibble out of the bag," Dooley said apropos of nothing. "It's his big secret. He waits until he hears the sound of a new bag being ripped open, and he makes sure he's the first one on the scene, eating his fill."

"Dooley, that information was private," I said between two bites.

"Now that we're sharing secrets, I also have one," said Joey. She turned to Zoey. "I once took one of your bones and hid it. I don't know why I did it. It was a spur-of-the-moment kind of thing. You'd just arrived to live with us and Ona had bought a nice big bone for me and a nice big bone for you, and I took both."

"I thought you said a bird got in and took it?" said Zoey, surprised.

Joey looked a little shamefaced. "No bird got in. I did it. It was me."

"That's all right," said Zoey. "I guess you thought I might take your place."

"You think?"

Zoey shrugged. "It's common knowledge that when pet parents adopt a new pet the older pets get nervous about being replaced or sidelined." She gave her friend a pat on the shoulder and added emphatically, "I forgive you, Joey."

"I wouldn't do that kind of thing now, of course. We're friends now."

"I know. And I've got my own secret."

"What secret?"

"I once put a piece of poop in your bowl. And you ate it."

Joey blinked a couple of times. "Uh-huh," she said finally.

"You weren't all that nice to me in the beginning, and so

one day I got a little upset about something you said so I pooped in your bowl. I figured you'd notice and get the message. But instead you ate it."

Joey made a slight retching sound. "I did, did I?"

"Yes, you did. You even said the food tasted better than usual."

"So maybe you should always eat poop from now on," Dooley suggested.

Joey made some more sounds as if she had a fishbone in her throat that wouldn't come out, but finally saw the humor in the situation. "It's fine," she said. "I know I wasn't very nice to you in the beginning, so I got what I deserved."

"You did hide my bone," Zoey reminded her.

"I did hide your bone. And you pooped in my bowl. Which means we're even."

They shared a glance, and burst out laughing. "What a pair we are!" said Zoey.

"You can say that again!" returned Joey.

While this heart-to-heart was going on, Dooley and I had polished off the bowls that had been on display, and I was feeling in excellent mood. "Why don't you tell us about your secret, Dooley?" I suggested.

But Dooley gave us a sheepish look. "I would, if I had a secret to share."

"Oh, come on, Dooley," said Joey. "Everyone has a secret."

"Except that I used to poop in the rose bushes, I don't really have any big secrets. I've never done anything really wicked or anything bad to anyone."

"It's true," I confirmed. "Dooley is just about the nicest cat in the world."

"I wish I had a secret," said Dooley fervently. "But I don't have one. One of our housemates has a secret, though. Harriet? But she doesn't want to tell us. We think she's having an affair with Kingman, who lives in town. Which is a big secret, since it might mean that either Harriet will move out, or Kingman will move in and Brutus will move out. Unless they want to have a *ménage à trois*."

I stared at my friend. "I didn't know you knew what a *ménage à trois* was?"

"Kingman explained it to me last night. He said it's Wilbur's most fervent wish one day to have a *ménage à trois* with two supermodels. And when I asked him what a *ménage à trois* is, he said it's like when people share an apartment? Like in *Friends*? Chandler and Joey living together, or Monica and Rachel?"

"Roommates," Joey confirmed. "Just like me and Zoey."

"Wouldn't that be nice, Max?" said Dooley. "That Kingman would come and live with us in a *ménage à trois*? Then we would be five instead of four."

"*Trois* is three in French," said Zoey. "So if there's five of you, it would be more like a *ménage à cinq*. *Cinq* is five in French," she explained.

"I just hope Harriet and Brutus can fix their problems," I said with a sigh.

I like Kingman, really I do, but he does have a habit of throwing his weight about to some extent. I simply couldn't imagine him and Brutus living under the same roof in peace and harmony. Pretty soon the same kind of behavior Joey and Zoey had described would be taking place in our home: with Kingman pooping in Brutus's bowl, and Brutus paying him in kind by returning the defecatory favor.

It wouldn't be pretty!

CHAPTER 18

We met up with Odelia and Chase in the corridor, where the latter stood conferring with the former. Apparently Chase had managed to get in touch with the detective tasked with following Jason Rocamora around, and had received a full report for his troubles.

"He was here all right," Chase was saying. "Parked right in front of the house. And guess who else was in the car?"

"Alison Droba?"

"Bingo. Dropped him off outside and then waited for him in the car. Rocamora then snuck up to the house, only to return ten minutes later, in a terrible hurry."

"What time was this?"

Chase wiggled his eyebrows triumphantly. "A little after two o'clock! Looks like we've got our man, babe!"

"Was he carrying something in his hands when he came out?" asked Odelia.

"Like what? Oh, you mean the laptop. I'll have to ask the guy. He snapped plenty of pictures, so if he was carrying

Isobel's valuables, he'll have photographic evidence." They headed for the stairs. "Oh, and guess what?"

"There's more?"

"You bet. So Isobel hired this agency to keep an eye on Rocamora, right? But Alison also hired the same agency to track down her father."

"Isn't that a conflict of interest or something?"

"I don't think it works like that for private investigators. And anyway, Isobel hired them to spy on Alison's boyfriend, not Alison herself."

"So did they find him? Alison's dad?"

"Not yet. They think he must be holed up in Mexico someplace. But it's a different detective handling that case from the one tailing Rocamora, obviously."

"Obviously."

We headed down the stairs, and I could tell that Chase was jubilant. Solving a murder case in just a couple of hours. It just might be a personal record for him.

"I already talked to your uncle. He's having Rocamora picked up as we speak."

"Good. I'm curious what he has to say for himself."

We left the house and walked back to Chase's car. Once we were on our way to town, I told Odelia about the various secrets we'd discovered. The one about Joey and Zoey didn't interest her as much as Ona's did, though. Which was understandable. Humans are mainly interested in other humans. Whereas pets are more interested in other pets. It's a common bias in all species.

She related the information to her husband, who nodded thoughtfully. "So Ona is nervous about her big secret coming out. I wonder how many others are in the same situation."

"They might all be in the same situation," said Odelia. "Even my mom and dad were acting really weird, so they might have some secret to hide as well."

"It all adds to Rocamora's motive. The more secrets are on that laptop, the more valuable it becomes, and the stronger the guy's motive for killing Isobel."

It was a sound piece of reasoning, and because my belly was full, I wasn't all that keen on disputing Chase's train of thought. If he thought Rocamora was our guy, he was our guy.

❦

Alison Droba was having a bad day. Probably the worst day of her life. And she knew something about bad days. Seven years ago her dad had murdered her uncle—or at least was involved in Uncle Dean's death—and had subsequently fled the country, afraid to be caught and sentenced to prison for manslaughter. It was something she'd had to live with for the past decade, and since the Drobas were such a prominent family, she hadn't even been able to process what had happened and try to put it behind her. The internet was filled with theories about what exactly had happened that night, and sightings of Gavin Droba. It seemed like he'd been seen everywhere by now, from Tahiti to Belgium to the North Pole.

Which is why she'd decided to hire that detective and put the stories to rest once and for all. If her dad was out there, they'd find him, she was sure about it.

And now this. First two police officers had showed up, informing her that her mother had been killed. And about an hour later, they'd returned to arrest Jason, accusing him of murdering her mother! This was a nightmare!

"You can't do this!" she screamed at the policewoman who was putting handcuffs on Jason's wrists.

"It's all right," said Jason.

"You have no right!"

"I'll be fine. Just get me a good lawyer, will you?"

"They can't do this to us," she said. "They just can't!"

"Yes, they can. They're the police, and I'm a suspect."

"But you didn't do nothing."

"Exactly. The truth will out, sweetie. And they'll have to let me go."

"Oh, God. Why does this keep happening to us!"

They led Jason to a police vehicle and put him in the back. He waved at her, his hands handcuffed, and giving her a reassuring smile.

She waved back at him, tears streaming down her face. And to think that the last time she and her mom spoke she'd said such terrible things to her. Telling her she was the worst mom in the world. And how she was going to get back at her for doing what she did. And all because Mom didn't approve of Jason. Of course she didn't. Jason had done time, and Mom found out about it, and had thrown a hissy fit. She would have settled down eventually. All she had to do was meet Jason and she'd see how silly she was being. How great Jason was, and so much not a criminal at all. They were going to sit down like grown-ups and talk this through. But instead she'd yelled at her mom, calling her names, and walked out.

And now she was gone. She'd never be able to apologize. To make up. To tell her she understood. That she was simply looking out for her little girl. Not wanting her to get involved with someone she saw as this dangerous delinquent.

"I get it, Mom," she said softly. "I get it now."

But it was too late. Mom was gone. Forever.

CHAPTER 19

Jason Rocamora was a handsome man. I would have put his age at late twenties, early thirties, which meant he was a few years Alison Droba's senior, as she was only twenty-one. He had a thick head of dark hair, a strong chin, and eyes that were almost black and stared back at Chase with undeniable defiance.

The two men were sitting opposite each other in the small interview room at the police precinct, with Odelia, myself and Dooley, and Uncle Alec watching on.

"I feel confident we've got our man in there," the Chief growled. "Good work."

Odelia didn't seem so sure herself, judging from the frown marring her otherwise smooth alabaster brow. But we'd soon find out from the interview.

"I had nothing to do with this and you know it," the reformed criminal opened proceedings. "I wasn't anywhere near the place last night!"

"So where were you, Jason?" asked Chase.

"In bed, with my fiancée. Ask her. She'll tell you."

"Oh, but we will," Chase assured the man. "Tell me about

this engagement with Alison Droba, will you?"

"What's there to tell? We love each other, Alison and me, and we're getting married as soon as the paperwork is done and the church is booked."

"Marrying in church, are you?"

"It's what Alison wants. Me, I don't care where we get married. But I love her, and I want to do right by her. So if Alison wants a big church wedding, she'll have it."

"And what about Alison's mom? She wasn't too keen on this wedding, was she?"

Jason made a face. "That was just a misunderstanding. Alison was trying to get her to meet me so we could talk things through."

"Isn't it true that Isobel strongly objected to you dating her daughter because of your criminal past?"

Jason shrugged. "Like I said, that's a big misunderstanding. I made some mistakes, but that's all behind me now. I've paid for those mistakes, and left that life behind me. Alison knows this, and I'm sure that if her mother had agreed to meet, I could have convinced her of my intentions and she would have accepted me."

"So the fact that you were in prison for aggravated robbery wouldn't have stopped her from accepting you as her daughter's future husband?"

"Like I said, that's all in the past. And besides, that was a misunderstanding."

"There seem to be a lot of misunderstandings in your life, Jason."

He grimaced. "I'd call it a miscarriage of justice, but I know you people don't like that kind of talk."

"So now you're denying the charges that were leveled against you at the time?"

"Absolutely. And if you'd looked into my case you'd know all this." He directed an angry look at his interrogator. "But then you don't care about the truth, do you? If you did, I wouldn't be sitting here, being accused of something I didn't do."

"Okay, so let's go back to last night. You claim you were at home with Alison when her mother was being killed."

"I don't claim this, I was there. We never left the apartment."

"So if a witness says they saw you getting out of Alison's car at two o'clock last night, and walk up to the house where Isobel was staying, they'd be lying, is that it?"

Jason became weary. "Who's the witness?"

"Let's just say the statement is credible."

"Then I'll say he's lying. Flat out lying."

At this moment Chase placed a number of photographs in front of Jason, and I could see his composure crumbling. He was shuffling nervously on his chair, and had turned a little white around the nostrils.

"For the tape, I'm showing Mr. Rocamora a series of photographs taken last night at two o'clock, clearly picturing him leaving a car driven by Alison Droba, and walking up to the house where Isobel Droba was staying. You can see Alison behind the steering wheel, and you in her presence."

"I-I can explain this," said Jason, and swallowed nervously.

"Please do," said Chase. "Cause I'd say you've been lying to me."

"I was there," said Jason. "That's to say, we were there."

"And what were you doing there?"

"Look, Isobel and Alison had a big fight that afternoon, all right? And so we figured that I'd talk to her and try to make her see reason."

"And you thought you'd do this in the middle of the night?"

"Sure. Isobel was always working late on that book of

hers. And when I walked up to the house I saw the light was still on in her room. Also, I didn't want to bump into Michele —that's Alison's aunt."

"And why is that?"

"Because she hates me even more than Isobel did," said Jason with a touch of bitterness. "Absolutely detests me, Detective, for no good reason except she's filled with some kind of prejudice, even though we've never even met. But anyway, so Alison thought it might be a good idea if I met Isobel face to face, without anyone else present, and so she dropped me off after midnight last night."

"Two o'clock, as the time stamp on these photographs clearly indicate."

"Okay, fine, two o'clock. So I go up to the house, and I see that the light in her room is still on."

"How did you know where Isobel's room was?"

"Alison had told me. She drew me a diagram. I had it in my hand as I was approaching, as you can see here." He was pointing to one of the pictures, and Chase checked and nodded. "Okay, so I see that her light is still on, and I shimmy up the drainpipe, which Alison said would get me straight to her mother's room."

"You didn't think she'd be scared when she suddenly saw your face appear at her window? Especially as she knew you were a convicted criminal she'd warned her daughter about?"

"That couldn't be helped. Alison had suggested a meeting many times, but her mom kept refusing. Said she wanted nothing to do with me—I blame Alison's aunt for that. She's the one who kept badmouthing me to her sister. But anyway, so I finally reach her window and I look in. And that's when I saw it."

"You saw what?"

"Isobel. She was lying there, and it was obvious that she was dead."

"How did you know? Did you climb in and check her pulse?"

Jason gave Chase a look that said 'Are you kidding me?' "She was dead, man. No doubt about it. There was blood everywhere, and her head was bashed in."

"So what did you do? Did you call an ambulance? Did you notify the police?"

"I ran. I got out of there as fast as I could."

"Now why is that, you think?"

"Because I knew that if I stuck around you'd blame this thing on me! And it wouldn't be the first time either! Once a criminal, always a criminal, right?"

"So you ran back to the car and told Alison what happened to her mom?"

"I did, yes. And then I told her to get out of there as fast as possible."

Chase rearranged his bulk on the chair and leaned forward. "I'm putting it to you, Jason, that you're lying to me again, just like you did at the beginning of this interview."

"I'm not, man—I'm telling you the truth, I swear!"

"I put it to you that you scaled that windowsill, climbed in through the window, and surprised Isobel. She started screaming and you panicked. So you hit her with the first object that you found, and then stabbed her until you were sure she was dead. And then you ran and told Alison some cock and bull story about finding her mother already dead and being afraid of being falsely implicated." He slammed the table with a meaty fist. "Isn't that the truth, Jason! Confess, son!"

"No! I didn't do it, sir. I swear. I'm being set up—just like I was that time."

Chase leaned back and studied the ex-con through slitted eyes. "I don't believe you. I'm sorry but I don't. And I don't think a judge or jury will believe you either."

"Oh, God, no. Not again!" said Jason whiningly. "This isn't happening!"

"But it is happening, Jason. So you better tell me the truth. Don't you want to spare your fiancée the pain and suffering of not knowing what happened to her mom? Don't you want her to know what happened, exactly?"

Jason became explosive, and now pounded his own fist on the table. "Of course I want her to know. But I didn't do it, all right?!"

"All right, all right," said Chase appeasingly. "Settle down."

"I looked in through the window, but I never set foot inside that room, I swear. I didn't touch anything. I was never in that room. And if you know your business you'll find that I'm telling you the truth. You won't find any fingerprints or DNA anywhere, and that's because I was never there. I didn't touch the woman!"

"Okay, so let's assume just for a moment that you're telling the truth. What else did you see? Cause you must have arrived right on the heels of the murder."

"I didn't see anyone. Apart from Isobel lying there, I didn't see anyone else."

Chase's face, otherwise so impassive, was now working. It was obvious that he didn't believe a word this young man was saying. But how was he going to get him to confess? It seemed impossible, as he was sticking to his story, no matter what.

"Okay, let's take a break," he said finally.

"Can I go home now?" asked Jason.

"I'm afraid not, son."

The young man's expression hardened. "Then I want a lawyer."

"Of course you do," said Chase, and left the interview room.

CHAPTER 20

We were in Uncle Alec's office, the adults in the room discussing the interview with Jason Rocamora, while Dooley and myself were relegated to the role of passive bystanders. But then isn't that often the case? People don't appreciate the value the feline point of view can bring to any conversation, now do they? Odelia sometimes appreciates my input, or Dooley's, but both Chase and Uncle Alec have in the past often been dismissive of our unique contribution to their cases.

"I think we've got our man," Chase reiterated. He was balling his fists, as if prepared to go mano a mano with anyone who dared to contradict his position. "He did it. I can feel it in my bones. Now all we have to do is make him confess."

"It does feel like a shoo-in," Uncle Alec confirmed. "He's got the motive, he had the opportunity, and he's got that violent past. But where is the murder weapon?"

"Oh, we'll find it," Chase assured the Chief. "I've got officers combing through every inch of the guy's apartment, and Alison Droba's car. We're bound to find the evidence we need to get a conviction." He was balling his fists again. "Just give me another couple of days with the guy, Chief. I know I can break him. I just know it."

"Let's just take it easy, shall we?" said the police chief. "I want a confession as badly as you do, but if we can get him on the evidence, that's just as good."

"What about Alison?" asked Odelia. She'd been pensive throughout.

"What about her?" asked her partner.

"If Jason killed her mother, why is she defending him? Insisting he's innocent?"

"Because she's in love with the guy, that's why!" said Chase. "She'd say anything to get him off the hook."

"But Isobel was her mother, Chase. Even if she loves Jason, what he did is indefensible—if he's guilty."

"You're absolutely right," said Chase, pounding his hand with his fist. "I should have arrested her alongside her boyfriend. If he's guilty, so is she. She knew he did it, and helped him conceal the evidence—at the very least. Chances are she was in on it. Encouraged him to get rid of her mother so they could get married and stop her mom from cutting her off financially."

"What do you mean?" asked the Chief.

"Well, now that Isobel is out of the way, Alison will inherit, won't she?"

"You think the two of them planned this together? Cold-blooded murder?"

"Of course! Bonnie and Clyde got nothing on this couple. Oh, they're cold, all right. Cold and cunning." He sprang up from his chair like a coiled spring. "I better nail her before she tries to get away."

And before they could stop him, he was out the door.

"I don't know about this," said Odelia. "Rocamora sounded very convincing."

"Psychopaths always do," said Uncle Alec. "Now get lost, will you? And get me the evidence I need to wrap this case up nice and neat!" he added as Odelia left the office, Dooley and me in tow.

"What do you think, Max?" asked Dooley once we were out on the street again, and on our way to Odelia's car. "Did he do it? Along with his girlfriend?"

"I don't know, Dooley," I said. "He does seem like the perfect candidate, doesn't he? He must have hated Isobel for her refusal to grant her blessing for the wedding. And now with her out of the way he'll get his wedding and the benefit of a very large family fortune. That's an excellent motive for murder. And let's not forget he has confessed to being on the scene when the murder was committed. We even have photographic evidence and a witness who saw him there."

"It does look very bad for him, doesn't it? And for his girlfriend."

"It does," I agreed. Which meant that this case could be wrapped up today.

"Not so nice for Alison, though," said Dooley. "If she was involved, she'll go to prison, and if she wasn't involved, her boyfriend just killed her mother."

"Yeah, that wedding is definitely off, I'd say."

We hopped into the back of Odelia's aged pickup, and settled in for the duration. Since the backseat of the car is mostly used by the four of us, its smell is very familiar, and very pleasing to a cat's sensitive nose. And so I dug my nails into the nylon cover while Odelia pulled the car into traffic and we were on our way.

"Where are we going?" asked Dooley.

"The coroner's office," Odelia informed us. "Abe asked us

to drop by. And now that Chase is busy arresting Alison Droba, I guess it's up to us to do the honors."

I swallowed away a lump of uneasiness. I don't like the coroner's office. It's very creepy, with dead people stuffed away in fridges, and Abe Cornwall cutting open dead bodies like some benevolent butcher. Not exactly my kind of place!

"We don't have to watch as he cuts open a person, do we?" I asked.

Odelia smiled at us in the rearview mirror. "You can stay in the car if you want."

"Good." But then I thought better of it. What kind of a feline sleuth would I be if I allowed my humans to do all the hard work, while I lounged around in cars? "Or maybe we'll tag along," I said finally. "But we might wait in the corridor."

"Suit yourself," said Odelia, then lapsed into thought as the car ate up the miles.

"I don't want to see more dead bodies, Max," said Dooley quietly. "I've seen one, and that's about all I can stomach for a day. My ration reached, you know."

"Same here, buddy," I said. "So let's agree now that when we spot a dead body, we'll take cover, all right?"

"Deal," said Dooley, well pleased with my sensible approach to the matter. "We'll hide under Abe's desk the moment he starts trotting out dead bodies."

CHAPTER 21

Fortunately for us Abe received us in his tiny office. Of dead bodies there was no trace, but documents piled high on his desk were plenty. Also present was a skeleton, located in a corner of the office, grinning at us with malevolent delight.

"I'll keep an eye on that skeleton, Max," Dooley assured me. "And if it makes a move, I'll scream, all right?"

"Good thinking, Dooley," I said. Even though I didn't think that skeleton had a lot of life left in its bony limbs, a careful cat is prepared for any contingency.

"I can see what you're thinking," said Abe once he'd lowered his voluminous corpus in the chair behind his desk. He adjusted his glasses and gave Odelia a quizzical look. "And you're absolutely correct. But I have my reasons."

"What am I thinking?" asked Odelia, amused.

"You're thinking: why did I have to come all this way out here, if you could have sent me your report through the swift powers of the internet?"

"You're right. That's what I was thinking," Odelia confirmed.

"The thing is that my report is in need of some explanation."

"Well, let's have it then," said Odelia, settling in.

"It hasn't moved yet, Max," Dooley told me. He was keeping a close eye on that skeleton. "So far so good."

"Okay, so as I thought, the cause of death was blunt force trauma to the back of the head—more in particular the occipital bone. The weapon you're looking for would most likely be some blunt object. Could be a baseball bat, candlestick—something smooth and heavy. So that is what killed her. But what I wanted to talk to you about are these." He had turned his computer screen, and a series of gruesome pictures now appeared.

I had to look away, but Odelia seemed transfixed.

"What are they?"

"At first glance I thought they were a series of knife wounds. But on closer inspection these couldn't have been produced by a knife. A sharp object, yes, but not sharp enough to create a clean entry wound. The wounds are frayed, as you can see here and here and here."

"I see," said Odelia, even though I didn't. "So what did the killer use?"

Abe leaned back, folding his hands across his rotund belly. His hair was practically fizzing with satisfaction. "Stiletto heel," he said finally, rolling the words around his tongue like a wine connoisseur would a nice Beaujolais.

"Stiletto heel?"

"Stiletto heel," the coroner confirmed. "As you can see there are footprints present, made when the perpetrator dug the heel of a stiletto deep into the chest."

"God."

"God had nothing to do with this, Odelia. Man did. Or a woman, of course."

"Men don't wear stilettos."

Abe arched a meaningful furry eyebrow. "Don't they? Anyway, that's for you to decide. I'm simply presenting you with the evidence. You use it to nab the maniac who first clubbed this woman to death, then mistook her chest for a pincushion."

"Is it possible that the killer grabbed a stiletto and used it on the victim?"

"You mean without actually wearing it?" He shook his head. "Out of the question. The depth of these wounds, and the marks on the chest suggest a great deal of force used. Which suggests that they were made by pressing down on the chest with a foot, not a hand. Unless the person was remarkably strong, of course. But even so. The evidence points to a frenzied attack by someone pressing their foot down several times. I've counted no less than a dozen separate wounds."

"So… would a woman be capable of using this kind of force?"

"Of course. The leg muscles are capable of producing a lot of force, whether male or female."

"This seems to suggest a great deal of rage, wouldn't you say?"

"It does have all the hallmarks of a particularly frenzied attack."

"We have a suspect in custody right now," Odelia explained. "An ex-con. I was thinking he could have knocked down Isobel, then his fiancée could have finished the job by hitting her with her foot. Is that possible, you think? Two perpetrators working in tandem?"

"Of course. But you'll appreciate such conjecture is beyond my area of expertise. One suspect or two—that's something for you and your husband to work out."

As Odelia got up, and extended her hand, Abe shook it warmly. "I have to say I had my doubts about you and Chase working as a team. You being a reporter and all, and having enjoyed no formal training. But by all accounts you're doing fine."

"My uncle seems to think I have something of value to add," Odelia said modestly. "He says I bring a human touch to the investigation. Cause people to open up. Not sure if that's true or not."

"And we bring the feline touch, don't we, Max?" said Dooley.

"That, we do," I said as we took our leave.

"So how is little Grace?" asked Abe as he led us through the warren of corridors that constitute the county coroner's lair.

"She's doing great, actually," said Odelia. "My grandmother dropped her off at the daycare center this morning—or at least I hope she did."

"Not getting dotty in her old age, is she? Though one might argue Vesta has always been dotty." He laughed at his little joke, while Odelia merely smiled.

We'd told her how Gran seemed to have forgotten that Grace was at the daycare center the day before, and it had caused Odelia some measure of concern.

Once we were back in the car, and on our way to Hampton Cove, she said, "Has Gran been acting strange again? Or was it just the one time, you think?"

"I think she's fine," I said, not having noticed anything out of the ordinary, apart from the one slip.

"Maybe she just woke up from a nap," Dooley suggested. "We all get confused when we wake up from a nap. I know I do. Sometimes I don't know where I am."

"Mh," said Odelia, not entirely convinced.

And I understood where she was coming from. She often entrusted Grace to Gran for babysitting duties, and if the old lady was going batty, perhaps that wasn't such a good idea.

But soon Gran was forgotten when Odelia's phone chimed. She put it on speaker and said, "Yes, babe? Did you make the arrest?"

"I thought I'd wait until we got confirmation from the crime scene people. They've been going through Alison's car, and the apartment she shares with Jason."

"And?"

"Nothing. Zip. Nada. Not a single drop of blood or hair of the victim or sign of the murder weapon. And the car hasn't been cleaned recently either."

"I see."

"If Jason had killed Isobel, you'd expect him to have blood on him, wouldn't you? And if he got back into the car, that blood would be on the car seat, since that detective says he saw the guy get into the car with Alison and take off."

"Did you talk to that detective again? Double-check if Alison stayed put?"

"I did, and he's adamant. Alison never got out of that car, and Jason was only gone ten minutes, and when he got back there wasn't a trace of blood on him."

"Something else is going on," said Odelia. "I talked to Abe Cornwall, and according to him we're looking for two murder weapons: a club and a stiletto."

"Stiletto like in a stiletto knife?"

"No, a shoe."

Odelia explained in a few words what the coroner had told her, and Chase sounded as surprised as she had been in Abe's office. It seemed incongruous, of course: a perpetrator who used both a heavy club and a stiletto heel to murder.

"Must be two different people," Chase said finally. "A man and a woman."

"Jason Rocamora and Alison Droba," said Odelia.

"Exactly."

They were both silent for a moment, then Chase

expressed his anger in a colorful way by referring to the private detective in not-so-friendly terms. I would have covered Dooley's ears but unfortunately it was too late. In real life, just like in live broadcasting, sometimes you just wish they'd institute a five-second delay!

CHAPTER 22

Ona was pacing her room, feeling restless and unhappy. At first so pleased that Michele had invited her to this tennis retreat, now she knew she should never have said yes. She hardly knew these people, and with this whole murder business she had the impression they were looking at her, the outsider, as a possible suspect for the death of this woman.

Max didn't seem to mind. He even enjoyed all the excitement the presence of the police had brought. He liked to watch crime shows of an evening, and now that he found himself in the middle of one himself, he was thrilled, chatting to the cops at every possible opportunity so he could collect stories and relate them later to his friends. He'd confided in her he might even turn it into a book.

He loved reading detective fiction, and had long held the belief he could churn something out himself if he only set his mind to it. And now life had landed a big juicy murder case in his lap. Surely it was a sign from the universe that he was the next Michael Connelly or Jeffery Deaver?

But for Ona this wasn't a game. It wasn't fun or exciting.

Instead she found the whole situation of staying on at this place simply terrible and nauseating. Already she'd been sick that morning, and her stomach still wasn't how it should be. She'd caught a glimpse of the dead woman, and every time she remembered, the nausea returned. She might have to go and see her therapist. She could have suffered major emotional trauma.

She stared out the window for a moment, which offered a view of the tennis courts, and saw that others weren't as adversely affected as she was: Perlita and Nathan Gruner were actually engaged in a game of tennis. How could they! At a time like this? When the blood of that poor Isobel was still staining the carpet in her room? Some people were so insensitive.

And as she turned back from the window with disgust, her eyes were suddenly drawn to the door, where an envelope was lying.

Joey and Zoey had also discovered this, for they sat next to the pristinely white envelope, and yapped with pleasant anticipation.

"What's this?" she said as she knelt down and picked it up.

There was no name on the envelope, but she assumed it was addressed to her. Why else would someone have slipped it under the door of her room?

She opened the envelope and found a small piece of paper tucked inside.

The moment she read the words, she gasped in shock. Her violently shaking hands were no match for the unadulterated evil contained in that short message, and piece of paper and envelope fluttered from her fingers to the floor, where they were greeted with pretty excitement by her two canine companions.

After much debate, Chase had decided to allow his most promising suspect to walk free. He might still be the most likely person to have killed Isobel Droba, along with his accomplice Alison, but the evidence simply wasn't there. The fact of the matter was that he couldn't have done it, unless the private detective who'd been watching the couple was also an accomplice, which seemed unlikely, and that somehow they'd magically been able to remove every single trace of the crime from their person and from the car. Also: no murder weapon was found at Jason's apartment, and no sign that Alison might be involved in the crime. And no bloodied clothes or shoes, though they could have dumped them, of course.

So it was back to square one for the investigation, and we were back at the house, for more interviews with potential suspects—which now included every person at the house. Officers were going through the rooms, and searching the grounds and tennis courts, looking for one heavy blunt instrument and one stiletto shoe, as used in the perpetration of last night's heinous crime.

"This is just outrageous," Chase fumed. "Two perfectly good suspects, and we can't connect them to the crime. How stupid is that?"

We were waiting in the living room for Michele Droba to join us. Chase's new line of inquiry was the book Isobel was writing, implicating one of her friends in some compromising situation that they were desperate to avoid being revealed.

Michele entered the room looking slightly annoyed. "I thought you had your suspect in custody for Isobel's murder? Rocamora? He must have killed her."

"Unfortunately the evidence doesn't seem to bear that out," Chase grudgingly admitted. "Which is why we wanted to talk to you again, Mrs. Droba. As we see it, the reason your sister-in-law was killed must be the book she was writing."

"Oh, so now we're back to this book, are we?" said Michele, as she took a seat on the cream-colored leather sofa, gracefully crossing her legs and leaning back.

"Isobel must have talked to you about it," said Odelia. "She must have revealed some of its contents. Is there anything you remember that could be connected to her death?"

"Nothing," said Michele. "Isobel knew I didn't approve of her writing that book of hers, and the only times we discussed it was when I told her to stop writing it, and she flatly refused."

"So she never told you what was in the book?"

"Never."

"She didn't tell her publisher? Your boyfriend?"

"You can ask him, but as far as I know they never talked about the content. Chris had given Isobel *carte blanche* to write whatever she wanted."

"Wasn't that unusual for a publisher to give a writer that much freedom?"

"Unusual, maybe. But it was the only way Isobel agreed to work. If Chris had told her he wanted the editorial prerogative to cut parts of the book, she wouldn't have signed the contract. She was going to write the book the way she wanted to, whether we liked it or not—and that included her publisher."

"But there would have been a scandal," said Chase.

Michele laughed. "Well, that was the whole idea! Publishers thrive on scandal, detective. Scandal sells, and that was what he was hoping for. If anything, he was nervous about the book being too tame. A lot of hullabaloo had been caused when the book was announced, and he hoped the final product would live up to it."

"That must have been very upsetting for you," said Odelia.

"Yeah, didn't that make you angry with Christopher?" asked Chase. "That he would prefer to make a lot of money from Isobel's book over your desire for discretion and protecting your friends' privacy?"

A fine smile played about the woman's lips. "Of course I was upset with Chris, but I also understood where he's coming from. A publisher is in the business of making money, detective. Otherwise he's not a very good publisher, is he? And I do admire his ambition to be successful at what he does. And as far as protecting my friends' privacy, well…" She made an ineffectual gesture. "That ship had sailed, I'm afraid. There was simply no turning back the clock on Isobel's book."

"What was the big secret Isobel was revealing about you?" asked Odelia.

"Like I said, I never got to read the book, and neither did Chris. But the only secret I ever revealed to Isobel was that I can't cook. So I'm sure that would have made its way into her book."

"You can't cook?"

"No, I can't," said Michele, smoothing her red gingham pants. "I would have liked to give people the impression that I'm some kind of Martha Stewart, but the truth is that I hate cooking. Whenever I throw a party, or organize something like this week, I always bring my housekeeper, who's an excellent cook. I know it's a silly thing, but I was hoping Isobel would leave it out of that book of hers. But knowing her, it would probably have been in the opening chapter."

"As secrets go, that's not exactly a shocker," said Odelia kindly.

"I know it doesn't seem like such a big deal, but when you present yourself as the perfect hostess, and you even run a lifestyle blog, it is embarrassing to admit that you cannot cook. But the fact of the matter is that it wasn't my own secret I was nervous about being revealed, but those of my friends and family."

"Can you tell us something about that?" asked Odelia.

Michele offered a fine smile. "I'm afraid I can't."

"Even if those secrets are what got Isobel killed?"

"Even if I knew some of these so-called secrets, I couldn't possibly betray a confidence. I'm sorry, but I simply can't. And besides, it's not my place to tell."

"Okay, fine," said Chase, though he didn't seem fine with it. "So tell me about your husband."

Michele frowned. "What do you mean?"

"Your husband Dean and his brother Gavin."

"I already told you. Dean died and his brother disappeared. But that has nothing to do with Isobel's murder."

"We'll be the judge of that," said Chase, a little nastily, I thought. Clearly he was in a foul mood: his perfect suspect slipping through his fingers, and Michele refusing to play ball were not conducive to softening his demeanor.

Michele sighed. "Okay, so one night seven years ago—"

"Where was this, exactly?"

"At the house—the house where Dean and I lived, and where I still live."

"So describe the scene for me, please."

"Dean had just returned home from work and was in his study making some phone calls when Gavin and Isobel dropped by. This must have been around eight or nine o'clock. Gavin was clearly agitated."

"You saw him? You were there?"

"I opened the door for them and told Gavin where he could find my husband, yes."

"Go on."

"Gavin had been drinking. I could smell the alcohol on his breath."

"Was that a common thing with him?"

"No, it wasn't. It was unusual." She played with the hem of her shirt. "I was in the kitchen with Isobel, chatting about this and that, when we suddenly heard a terrible noise. Crashing and the breaking of furniture. So we quickly made our way over to the study, and there he was, lying on the floor next to his desk: Dean had taken a bad fall, and hit his head against the corner of the desk. Gavin was in a real state, screaming that he'd killed his brother. So I called an ambulance, but by the time they arrived, Gavin was gone."

"Gone where?"

"The police later determined that he'd returned home, collected money and his passport, and had driven himself to East Hampton Airport, where he boarded the company's private jet to New York JFK, where he took a flight to Mexico. They lost track of him after that."

"And he's never been in touch with his wife or your family since?"

She shook her head. "Gone without a trace."

"Why was Gavin so upset with your husband that night?" asked Odelia.

"He never said, and obviously Dean couldn't tell us what happened, since he was declared dead by the first responders. But it must have had something to do with the company. You see, when Bill, my father-in-law, retired, he decided to put Dean in charge of the Droba Group, with Gavin as his second-in-command. His official title was CFO, Chief Financial Officer, while Dean was appointed CEO. And that never sat well with Gavin. He felt slighted and passed over by his dad, even though Dean was older and more experienced and had been with the company longer, since Gavin had enjoyed a gap year after college, and had traveled around the world while Dean had stayed home and worked for his dad all that time."

"Sibling rivalry," said Chase, nodding.

"Sad business, and not my family's finest hour, but there you have it. Though I still don't see what this could have to do with what happened to Isobel."

"Alison told us she hired a detective agency to track down her dad," said Odelia. "Is it possible that Gavin came back, and somehow killed his wife?"

"No way," said Michele. "Gavin and Isobel were a devoted couple. Gavin would never do anything to harm his wife. Did…" She hesitated. "Did this detective Alison hired find out what happened to Gavin?"

"Unfortunately no. But they're still looking."

"I see. Isobel never told me about this."

"She didn't know. This was Alison's idea. She wants to find her dad."

"Of course. She misses her dad. She was so young when it happened."

"Did Bill ever try to find his son?" asked Chase.

"Maybe he did. You'd have to ask him. He never mentioned anything to me. I guess he understood why Gavin would run away, after what happened to Dean."

"I checked, and he's still wanted for questioning in connection to the events that transpired that night. Which might be the reason he hasn't been in touch."

"It was an accident, detective. Gavin had no intention of causing Dean's death."

We all looked up when the sounds of a quarrel reached our ears. It sounded like a man and a woman fighting, and screaming at each other at the top of their lungs. Those present shared a look, then got up as one man, and hurried out.

CHAPTER 23

After finishing their doubles game against the Alemans, Vena and Glenn, Perlita had immediately returned to the room to take a shower while Nate decided to head down to the kitchen for a snack. And she'd just entered the room when Nate's phone buzzed and almost fell off the little piecrust table near the window. She nudged it back toward the middle of the table, and as she did, the message caught her eye. Stunned, she grabbed the phone to take a closer look.

And it was at that moment that her husband entered the room, a Snickers bar in hand, of which he'd already taken a big bite, and was chewing happily.

"What the hell!" she screamed, and threw the phone at his face.

He ducked just in time, causing the phone to hit the door with a thwack. "Hey!" he said. "Watch it!"

"Izzy Price?! You're cheating on me with Izzy?!"

Nathan's jaw dropped. "I'm—what are you talking about?"

"I saw the message, Nate. 'I'm naked and thinking of you?' What the hell, Nate!"

"I-I can explain," he said, holding up his hands in a gesture of defense, just in case she decided to throw something else at him. Like a table or a chair.

"How long has this been going on?" she demanded. "How long?!"

"Six months," he said sheepishly.

"Six months!"

He nodded, and carefully picked up his phone and checked to see if it still worked.

"I want a divorce," she said, causing him to blanch.

"But, honey!"

"Don't you honey me," she said, pointing a menacing finger at her husband. "You're having an affair with my main artist and your main client. How dare you!"

"You're one to talk," he scoffed. "Don't think I don't know what you've been up to."

She was momentarily taken aback by this comeback. "What are you talking about?"

"Izzy told me that you and her…" He gestured between them. "That you've… Well, that you've been… doing things together!"

She should have laughed at the prudish way he expressed himself. Nate hated talking about the more intimate side of their relationship, preferring to keep things under the covers—literally. It usually cracked her up. But she was too shocked now to even crack a smile. "What do you mean?" she asked feebly.

"You and Izzy, you're also having an affair, aren't you? So when were you going to tell me about that, huh?"

"I'm…" She gulped uncomfortably at this sudden reversal of the roles of accuser and accused. "It just… happened once. Once only. And it was a mistake." A mistake she had thoroughly enjoyed, though, and had been eager to repeat. Which is why she was so disappointed that Izzy was also carrying on with Nate. Somehow it made her feel doubly betrayed—by her husband and her lover.

For a moment they just stared at each other, then the door swung open and those detectives walked in, followed by Michele.

Perlita snapped, "I want to go home."

"I'm afraid you can't," said Detective Kingsley, as he checked to see if any damage had been done—either to the furniture or the people present.

"But I have to go home—I can't stay here one minute longer." And she couldn't. Not in the presence of this man, who'd betrayed her to such an extent. He knew she and Izzy had experienced a special moment, as she liked to call it, and still he chose to start an affair with her? It was sickening. Simply sickening.

"You can't go home yet, Perlita," said the Kingsley woman, who was a lot kinder than her cop husband it had to be said. "The investigation isn't over yet, and until it is, we need you all to stay put. Just for a little while longer."

She set her face in an expression of determination. "Then I want a different room. And I want a divorce," she added for Nathan's sake. "And I want you to drop Izzy as a client." As Nate shook his head, she added, "I'm dropping her exhibition."

"You can't drop the exhibit, honey," said Nathan. "It would end her career."

She tilted her chin in a defiant gesture. "She should have thought of that before she started her affair with you." And with these words, she swept from the room. Too late she remembered that all of her things were in that room. But she'd be damned if she went back as long as Nate was there. She'd sneak in when he was gone to grab her stuff.

She entered the first room she found and locked the door.

Then she sat down on the floor and broke down in tears. Tears for her marriage, but also for Izzy.

§

Chase and Odelia were taking a turn about the garden. To gather their thoughts and decide on the course of their investigation. Dooley and I trailed behind them, still discombobulated about recent events. After his wife had left the room, Nathan Gruner had told us what their fight had been about. It also stood to reason that this was the secret that might have made its way into Isobel's book.

"So Perlita Gruner was having an affair with Izzy Price," said Dooley. "While her husband was having an affair with Izzy Price. What a coincidence, don't you think, Max? That both husband and wife would be having an affair with a woman with the same name."

"I think you'll find that it's actually the same woman, Dooley." Which was also the reason the domestic contretemps had been so vociferous and so spiteful.

"The same woman? But how can that be?" asked Dooley.

"Obviously it's possible," I said, "for one person to be having an affair with two different people, in this case husband and wife."

"You mean like a *ménage à trois*? Like Harriet and Brutus and Kingman?"

"Something like that," I agreed. "Though we don't know if Harriet is having an affair with Kingman, and as long as we're not sure, we shouldn't assume Brutus's suspicions are correct."

"This Izzy Price person sure gets around," said Dooley with a touch of admiration in his voice.

Odelia and Chase had their own ideas about the whole

situation. Though their focus seemed to be on Gavin Droba, and not so much on the Gruners.

"Is it possible that one of the men in this place is actually Gavin Droba?" asked Chase now, suggesting a new and intriguing possibility. "That he returned from Mexico a long time ago, and inserted himself into his wife's circle of friends?"

"But wouldn't Isobel recognize her husband?"

"Not if he had some work done on his face."

"Plastic surgery, you mean?"

Chase gave a meaningful nod of the head. "What if Gavin Droba decided to return home, but not before thoroughly changing his appearance? Somehow or other he manages to finagle his way into Michele and Isobel's circle of tennis friends, and when the time is right, he strikes and kills her."

"But why? Michele said they were a devoted couple."

"Everyone thought the Gruners were a devoted couple, and look what happened. No, I don't buy this business about Gavin and Isobel being the perfect couple. I think Isobel was having an affair with Dean, and that's what that fight was all about. He shoved the man his wife was cheating on him with —his own brother—and Dean didn't survive the argument. Gavin fled, avoiding a painful trial and perhaps even jail time. He changed his appearance and returned to confront his wife. And in a fit of rage, he kills her."

"If Abe is correct the murderer was wearing stiletto heels."

"Could be that Gavin is a woman now."

"Oh, Chase."

"I'm serious! What better way to hide his real identity than to turn himself into a woman? Nobody would ever suspect him, and he'd get off his second murder in a decade scot-free. The perfect crime."

It was certainly food for thought. But then Odelia voiced

the perfect question: "If Gavin is here, then who is he? If what you're saying is true, he could be anybody."

"All we have to do to know for sure is to check the shoe sizes for all the ladies present. It can't be hard to narrow things down. And when we do, we've got him!"

"Or her."

CHAPTER 24

The search for a pair of stiletto heels was on, with Chase fervently hoping they would lead us to Isobel's killer. It was a long shot, to assume that Gavin Droba had returned as a woman intent on revenge, but then that's what being a detective is all about: sometimes you had to follow the evidence, and sometimes you had to let your imagination run wild, and hope it didn't lead you astray!

In the meantime the detecting duo doggedly pursued this line of inquiry by interviewing every person in that house. Next on the hot seat was Ona Konpacka, since we were focusing on the female members of the extended household now.

Ona was at the edge of her seat, literally, and seemed fidgety.

"No, I'm not Gavin Droba, detective," she assured us. "I've had operations done to my face, yes, but not because I used to be a different person. I've always been Ona, and the only reason I had extensive work done is because some butcher ruined my face when he injected me with some bad fillers." She glanced down at her hands, and added, softly, "And also my arms and thighs and chest." Suddenly big droplets of tears rolled from her eyes. "As far as your other question goes: yes, I did cheat my sister out of a career as a model. How did you find out?" But when Chase opened his mouth to speak, she quickly went on, "Don't tell me. You talked to Michele. I should stop confiding in people I hardly know. They don't seem to care about me." She took a big gulp of breath, then went on, "So yes, I'm a bad person. I stole my sister's career. I took her dream. In my defense, though, I made the best of things, and once I was launched in this business I discovered how much I liked it. And besides, who's to say my sister would have been successful? She might have stumbled at the first hurdle. This is not an easy life, detective. Not an easy career. I've had my highs as well as my lows. But what I haven't done is murder anyone. So no, I didn't kill Isobel Droba because she was about to reveal my big secret." She looked up. "I didn't do it. You have to believe me."

A police officer stuck his head in, and shook it in a vigorous no. No suspicious stilettos were found in Ona Konpacka's room. Unless she had discarded them, of course, which she would if she was the killer and if she was smart, which she was.

"Michele didn't tell us about your sister and the talent scout, Ona," said Odelia. She'd taken a seat next to the model on the sofa, and was rubbing her back consolingly. "I can't tell you who told us, but it wasn't Michele, all right?"

"Fine," said Ona between two sniffs. She'd gratefully accepted the tissue paper Odelia had handed her, and was dabbing at her eyes and nose now. "I'll ruin my skin," she lamented. "Max told me not to cry."

"Your boyfriend told you not to cry?"

Ona shrugged. "Everyone knows tears are bad for your skin. Too much salt."

"Well, I think one good cry won't hurt you."

"Easy for you to say," said Ona, giving Odelia a sideways glance. "You've got great skin."

"Why, thanks," said Odelia. "I guess if this detective thing doesn't work out, I could always go for a career as a model."

Ona laughed through her tears. "Better not. It's a pretty tough gig. I bet you wouldn't like it. I'm sure my sister wouldn't have liked it. So maybe I did her a favor."

"Maybe you did. What does she do, your sister?"

"She's a doctor. Brain surgeon. She's good. Very good."

"So maybe it's a good thing that she didn't become a model, right?"

"Yeah, maybe. But I don't like that she didn't have the option. I took that away from her, see? I didn't give her a choice. She's a great doctor, sure, but she might have had an amazing career as a model."

"Why don't you tell your sister? I'm sure she'll understand."

Ona gave her a deer-in-the-headlights look. "Are you going to tell her?"

"No, that's entirely up to you. We're not going to tell her anything."

She thought for a moment. "Mh. Yeah, I guess you're right. I've been carrying this with me for so long now, maybe it's time to finally tell her the truth."

Joey and Zoey had also entered the room, and jumped on Ona's lap now. She hugged the two doggies, and allowed them to lick her face.

"Why do they do that, Max?" asked Dooley.

"Do what?"

"Lick people's faces?"

"I think it's a sign of affection."

"Or maybe they like the taste of a human face?" He shivered. "Can you imagine having to lick Odelia's face all day? I don't care how affectionate it makes me seem, I don't want to ruin my appetite."

We both glanced up at Odelia, and I imagined licking her face. Not a pleasant prospect! I like Odelia, of course I do. But why would I want to lick her face?

"It's a sign of respect and affection," said Joey, who'd followed our conversation. "And besides, humans taste good, didn't you know?"

We both shivered some more, and regarded Joey in a different light. Taste good? Humans? What was this dog talking about? Was she related to Hannibal Lecter?

Which just goes to show how fundamentally different cats and dogs are. Whereas dogs like to slobber all over their humans, cats are respectful and fastidious. And let's not even mention the boundary issue. No one in their right mind likes to be attacked by some big drooling canine, people. Unless you're a so-called dog person, in which case you deserve everything that's coming to you.

CHAPTER 25

Back at the apartment Alison shared with Jason, the search had reached its conclusion. The upshot was that nothing of interest had been found. Alison's car had also yielded all of its secrets, which indicated that the couple had a fondness for takeout and the occasional bout of backseat nookie, but not for murder.

Chase and Odelia were on hand to escort Jason home. It was the least they could do now that he'd been found not to be guilty of murder, and when we arrived, Alison was waiting for us—or more likely her fiancé—with open arms.

Tears of happiness and joy were shed, but then Alison turned on us with a vengeance. Like her mother, she was dark-haired with an olive complexion, and green eyes that had a bewitching quality, especially now, when they were blazing with righteous fury.

"I told you he was innocent, and still you arrested him!"

"We had no other choice, Alison," said Odelia, whose bedside manner is a bit more gentle than her husband's, and whose task it is to calm suspects down. "Jason was right there when it happened, and he had a strong motive."

"And then there's his criminal record," said Chase morosely. He still hadn't ruled Jason out as a suspect, even though the evidence simply wasn't there.

"That criminal record is bogus," Alison insisted, balling her fists and practically stomping her feet.

We were standing in front of the building where they had their apartment. It was only three stories high, and all three apartments appeared similar in design. Jason and Alison occupied the top floor, where the last of the uniformed officers now descended the stairs, having finished their thorough search.

"What do you mean, bogus?" asked Odelia.

"Don't tell them," said Jason. "It's no use."

"It wasn't Jason who beat up that man. It was his brother Tim."

"Alison!"

"No, this needs to be said," the girl insisted. "Tim is old enough to fend for himself. You've looked out for him long enough. It's time you got some justice." Jason looked uncomfortable, but Alison wasn't to be deterred. "Tim was sixteen when he held up that liquor store. Him and his buddies. They hit that poor man over the head so bad he was in the hospital for months. He still walks with a limp. But since Timmy's mother would have been devastated if he was sent to juvenile detention, Jason said it was him that did it. That he robbed that liquor store. And so he was arrested and sentenced to prison for a crime he didn't even commit."

Chase and Odelia shared a look. "Why didn't you tell us this before?"

"Because I wanted to protect my brother," said Jason tersely. He refused to meet the detective's eyes. "You're not going to arrest him now, are you?"

Chase didn't reply. Instead he said, "So this is your secret? The secret Isobel was going to write about in her book?"

But Alison shook her head. "Mom didn't know. I never told her. I wanted to keep Jason's secret. But now that he's being charged with murder, we have to speak up." She thumped her fiancé's shoulder. "*You* have to speak up!"

"Only if it doesn't mean Timmy will be in trouble." He directed an anxious look at Chase. "Please don't arrest my brother. He was just a stupid kid, mixing with other stupid kids. He's turned his life around since this happened. Especially when I was sent to prison. He knows it should have been him. And it's made him think. And make a change. He stopped hanging out with those idiots. He cleaned up his act. And he's made something of himself. I'm proud of my brother."

"What does he do?" asked Odelia, clearly touched by Jason's story.

"He runs a construction company. Very successful, too. He's my boss now, since I work for him. I'm an electrician," he explained. "I learned in prison. My brother was the only one who wanted to hire me, which is ironic, as the reason I was in prison was to protect him. So now he's returning the favor by employing me."

It was a touching story, to be sure, but I could tell that Chase, for one, wasn't buying it. Alison must have noticed, too, for she thumped the cop's shoulder.

"Hey, what did you do that for!" the burly copper said.

"For arresting the wrong man. Twice!"

"I didn't arrest him the first time."

"No, he didn't," Jason confirmed.

"But you arrested him this time."

That was undeniable, but Chase was unapologetic. "He's still the most likely suspect," he insisted, which caused Alison to give him another shoulder thunk. "Stop that!" he warned. "Otherwise I'll have to arrest you for assaulting an officer."

"You wouldn't."

"Don't tempt him," said Jason as he glanced up at the cop.

"Okay, so there's one other thing I've been meaning to ask," said Odelia in an attempt to ease the tension. "This story about you hiring a private investigator to look for your dad, how did that work out? Did they find him?"

"Nothing so far, but I'm not giving up. I will find my dad."

"Have you ever considered that maybe your dad doesn't want to be found?" said Chase, rubbing his shoulder. "That maybe he had good reason to disappear?"

"What's that supposed to mean? He's still my dad. He wants me to find him."

"What Chase means is that your dad left the country for a reason. Because he was afraid he was going to be arrested for killing his brother," Odelia explained.

"I know all about that. But he didn't do it on purpose, did he? He gave my uncle Dean a shove, and he hit his head. It was an accident, and a good lawyer would get him off. So I don't understand why he doesn't come back to us."

"Maybe he has come back," said Chase, giving Alison a meaningful look.

The girl was quiet for a moment, then said, "I've been wondering about that. But when I mentioned this to my mom she said it was out of the question."

"So your mom knew about your search for your dad?" asked Odelia.

"Oh, sure. I told her all about it."

"And what did she say?"

"Surprisingly little. She seemed completely indifferent. Whether we found my dad or not didn't seem to matter to her one way or another. Which was odd."

"Odd, how?"

"As far as I can tell my mom and dad loved each other. But when I told Mom that I wanted to find him, and that I'd hired a detective, she simply didn't care."

"Another secret," Chase murmured. "So many secrets."

Alison looked up as if stung. "I'll have you know that every family has secrets," she said, stabbing his chest with a pointy index finger. "Better check your own closet for skeletons before you start digging into other people's."

"Hey, hey," said Odelia. "That's not what he meant."

"So what did he mean?" asked Alison angrily.

"That all the people involved in this case seem to be harboring secrets, and that your mother was collecting them, and was going to reveal them in her book. But she also had her own secrets, and that maybe one of them got her killed."

It gave the young woman food for thought. Finally she nodded. "Okay, I'm sorry. You're just doing your job, I know. But it's frustrating for me that you're accusing the people I love of things they didn't do."

"Well, that's too bad," said Chase, his jaw working.

"Oh, why do I even bother?" said Alison, and turned on her heel.

We watched her enter the apartment building, and Jason said, "She's feisty, isn't she? Which is probably why I love her so much." Then he seemed to realize he was talking to the people who had arrested him, and followed his fiancée in.

"Do you still think they did it?" asked Odelia after a few moments.

"Oh, yeah," said Chase. "I don't know how they did it, but they did it."

"One possibility is that they paid off that private investigator."

"I'm way ahead of you, babe. I've already ordered a background check on the guy. It's only a matter of time before we dig up the dirt on this crooked gumshoe. And then we've got them. All three of them. On conspiracy to commit murder."

CHAPTER 26

After a long day talking to witnesses and suspects, we were finally home again. But instead of resting on our laurels, as might be expected from a powerhouse detecting duo like myself and Dooley, we found ourselves in the midst of another mystery that needed our collective mental capacities. Or two mysteries, actually.

The moment we entered the house, Gran came hurrying up to us. She had a sort of wild look in her eyes, and asked, in a breathless way, "Grace! Have you seen Grace! Where is she!"

"She was at the daycare center all day," I informed Gran, as I watched her with a touch of concern. "Though now she's home again, since Odelia and Chase picked her up."

"But… where is she?" asked Gran. "Where is my great-granddaughter!"

Just then, Odelia walked in through the front door, Grace in her arms.

Gran seemed to relax at the sight of the little girl, but when I told Odelia later about what happened, she shared our concern.

"Maybe it's because she's all alone in the house," I suggested. "With Marge and Tex gone."

"Maybe," Odelia agreed. "We could invite her to stay with us, of course," she added with a tentative look at her husband, but Chase immediately shook his head. He might be fond of his grandmother-in-law, but not fond enough to have her under the same roof.

"She's got Harriet and Brutus," he said. "She's fine. And besides, she already spends all of her time here, and she's got a perfectly good bedroom next door. No need for us to fix up a room for her here."

He had a point, of course. Ever since Marge and Tex had left to hang out with their tennis buddies, Gran had spent her evenings with us, eating dinner with us, watching television with us, and staying up late until it was time to go to bed, which she did in her own room next door, where she had the company of Harriet and Brutus.

"I think she's simply disoriented," said Chase. "Without Marge and Tex, her life is a little out of whack right now. Once they're back, everything will be just fine."

"Let's hope so," said Odelia with a sigh. She had enough to worry about already, with her mom and dad involved in this murder inquiry, without having to worry about her grandmother going a little non compos, too.

And we'd just settled in on the couch, preparatory to taking a long pre-dinner nap, when Brutus came bursting in through the pet flap. "Max! Dooley! Where were you!" he cried. "Things have gotten so much worse while you were away!"

"We were at this tennis retreat with Marge and Tex," I said.

"A murder has been committed, and Marge and Tex are suspects," Dooley explained. "Though I don't think they did it. A retired crook did it, though he says he didn't do it, and his girlfriend swears he didn't do it, so now we don't know."

"Yes, yes, yes," said Brutus impatiently. "Who cares? It's Harriet you should be worrying about. She's having an affair with Kingman. I'm absolutely sure of it now. I've got proof!"

"You've got evidence of an affair?" I asked, intrigued. I like evidence. Evidence never lies, and it's a darn sight better than idle speculation, which seems to be rife in my line of work.

"Yes, I have!" said Brutus. I'd never seen him this excitable, and I didn't wonder.

"Well, what are you waiting for? Show us."

He led us out through the pet flap, into the backyard, and straight to the rose bushes at the bottom of the garden. "Smell," he said, once our small group had arrived.

"What?" I asked, not sure I'd heard him right.

"Smell!"

And so smell we did. We smelled here, we smelled there, we smelled everywhere. "Roses," I finally determined. "A little faint, but that's to be expected after a long day. I expect they'll smell much better in the morning."

"Not the roses, dummy!" Brutus cried. "It's Kingman! He was here!"

I frowned. Now cats are well-known and generally praised for their capacity to detect the presence of other cats by simply sniffing around a little and picking up their scent, but as far as I could tell those rose bushes didn't smell like Kingman at all. "Um… Are you sure?" I finally asked.

"Of course I'm sure. Can't you see? Harriet has been here with Kingman! In our own private little nook! She entertained that horrible poser in our nooky nook."

I refrained from asking what he meant by this phrase, but instead focused on the more vital matter of whether Kingman had indeed been there. I didn't think he had, but I wasn't going to contradict Brutus when he was in this frame of mind.

"I don't smell anything," Dooley finally revealed, after applying his nose in all directions. "Not Kingman, not Harriet, only roses and dirt."

"I think you'll find it's earth you smell, Dooley," I said. "Not dirt."

Dooley stuck his nose in the air and said, "I smell sausages, too."

The scent of sausages did indeed fill the air. Chase and Odelia were preparing dinner, which may have had something to do with that. And as I picked up the same smell, my stomach reminded me with a persistent rumble that I was hungry.

"Look, can we settle this Kingman business later?" I asked. "We haven't practically eaten anything all day, so…"

"We did eat those delicious nuggets offered by Joey and Zoey, didn't we, Max?"

"Yeah, but that was dog food, so that doesn't count." Well, it doesn't. Every expert will tell you that dog food lacks the necessary nutrients a healthy kitty needs. But then that's dogs for you. They put on a good show, but when it comes right down to it, they always let you down. "So let's have dinner first, shall we?"

Brutus, who was looking pretty down in the dumps, hung his head. "Oh, all right," he said moodily. "But I'm telling you that Kingman was here. In our own little spot. Our own little nooky nook."

"What's a nooky nook, Brutus?" asked Dooley as we headed back to the house.

"It's a spot where cats come to have nooky," he said before I could stop him.

"Okay, so what's nooky?" asked Dooley, his inquisitive mind never resting.

"Nooky is when two cats rub their noses together," I explained quickly.

"Oh, that's fun," said Dooley. "I like rubbing my nose against yours, Max." And to show us that he meant what he said, he demonstrated this sweet and innocent pastime by rubbing his nose against mine while saying, "Nooky nooky nook."

"Yes, nooky nooky nook," I murmured, catching Brutus's eye. The big black cat was shaking his head at this display of affection. Clearly he wasn't in the mood.

"I want you to talk to Harriet, Max," he said now. "And I want you to take a firm line this time. This kind of behavior has to stop."

"Harriet is a free woman, Brutus," I felt impelled to remind him. "If she wants to carry on with Kingman, she has every right." And even though I didn't think there was anything going on between Harriet and Kingman, clearly something was going on, and it was leading to Brutus experiencing a nervous breakdown.

"But there has to be something you can do, Max!" he cried helplessly.

"I'll talk to her," I promised him. "Again." Not that I thought it would do a lot of good. Clearly whatever secret Harriet was harboring was one she wasn't prepared to share with her friends and housemates. But it was certainly worth another try. Then I got an idea. "Why don't *you* talk to Harriet, Dooley?"

"Me? Talk to Harriet?" He made it sound as if I was asking him to walk the plank. Or to cross into the Amazon Rainforest and brave an ancient hostile tribe.

"Yeah. Harriet likes you. I have a feeling that she might open up to you."

"Harriet likes me?" He perked up at this.

"As a friend," Brutus growled warningly. "She strictly likes you like a friend."

"Oh, I knew that," said Dooley quickly. "Harriet and I are great friends."

"So talk to her like a friend," I suggested. "Try to find out what's going on."

"You mean, like a detective? Like Chase did today with that Rocamora person?"

"Something like that. Though try not to be as tough as Chase." Tough doesn't cut it with Harriet. She doesn't respond well to belligerence and bellicosity. The upshot might be that Dooley got his head bitten off, and we didn't want that.

CHAPTER 27

$\mathcal{D}$ooley liked Harriet, that much was certainly true. The fact that Harriet liked him was something new, though. In general he'd always seen her as a good friend, even though once upon a time he'd had fond feelings for her that might have been construed as deeper than mere friendship. But then the entire male cat population of Hampton Cove had harbored those types of feelings for the pretty Persian, so that was not exactly remarkable or surprising. And then of course Brutus had arrived on the scene, and that was that.

For a long time Brutus had been regarded as the third dog that runs away with the bone two other dogs had been fighting tooth and claw over. Only in this case the third dog was a strapping big cat, and the two other dogs had been about ninety-nine meeker cats, who had quickly accepted the new law of the land.

So when Dooley had taken on the mission to talk to Harriet and extract certain confidences from her, he wasn't entirely sanguine about the outcome. But when Max asked him to do something he always did it, because Max was his best friend, and Max was wise and Max knew, so it must be the right thing to do.

The fluffy Ragamuffin screwed up his courage and went in search of the equally fluffy white Persian. He didn't find her in the house, and he didn't find her in the backyard, nor did he find her in Marge and Tex's house, or in their backyard either. After a long search, he did find her one more backyard over, talking animatedly with Rufus and Fifi, the neighboring dogs—respectively belonging to Ted and Marcie Trapper and Kurt Mayfield, the retired music teacher.

The moment Dooley stuck his head through the fence, though, the lively conversation between the three pets abruptly halted, and an uncomfortable silence fell. To lift the tension, he did what any timid cat would do: he started babbling.

"Oh, hi, Fifi—Rufus," he said as he joined the trio, who regarded him with a touch of animosity. "Nice day, isn't it? The sun—very nice. The sky—very blue. Little white clouds —very cute. The weather report said we might have some rain tomorrow, though to be absolutely honest I don't put a lot of stock in the weather report anymore. They're often wrong, you know, even in this day and age of supercomputers and satellites. Have you eaten? I haven't eaten. Though I'm going to eat soon. Odelia is baking sausages, and I was hoping to get me some of those. Though sausages are meat, of course, and I'm a vegetarian. But Max says—"

"What do you want, Dooley?" Harriet interrupted the flow of words.

"Oh, nothing much," he said. "Just saying hello, you know. Shoot the breeze. Talk to my friends. You are my friends, you know. Fifi is my friend. And Rufus is my friend. And of course Harriet, you're my very good friend. Max says that friends don't keep secrets from their other friends, and so I was wondering if we could talk about our secrets. Just four friends talking about their secrets, you know. Like good friends do. I'll go first." He took a deep breath.

"I know what your secret is, Dooley," said Harriet before he could launch into his story. "I told you yesterday, remember?"

"You did?"

"Sure I did. And then Max told me that Brutus also has a secret, but he wouldn't tell me what it was. So are you finally ready to talk about that now?"

Dooley closed his mouth with a click. He didn't know Brutus's secret. What he did know was that the world is a commercial place. A big marketplace where trade is all that matters. You offer something and the other person offers something equally valuable of their own, and then you trade. And so if he wanted Harriet to divulge her secret, he'd have to come up with something equally valuable. Like Brutus's big secret—which as far as he knew didn't even exist!

His brain was buzzing with activity, his synapses firing on all cylinders. And then he had it. Bingo! "I know Brutus's secret," he revealed. "And even though Brutus has told me not to tell you, I will tell you. Because that's what friends do."

"Friends reveal other friends' secrets, even though they told you not to tell?" asked Fifi, arching a critical whisker in Dooley's direction.

This had him stumped for a moment, but then Harriet said, "Just tell me, Dooley." She had put a purr in her voice, and was regarding him from beneath lowered lashes, which she was flashing at him for some reason. The combination was pretty heady, he had to admit, and he was starting to feel a little weak-kneed.

"Well…" He'd totally forgotten what he was going to say —his mind a blank!

"I wouldn't tell her if I were you, Dooley," said Rufus after clearing his throat. The big sheepdog seemed serious. "Secrets are meant to be guarded, not revealed."

"Rufus, shut up," said Harriet.

"I'm just saying."

"Well, don't."

"Okay," said Dooley, thinking hard, even though his brain had turned into a clump of molasses.

"Tell me, Dooley!" Harriet insisted. The eyes that had regarded him so seductively less than a minute ago were now shooting twin bolts of lightning and she couldn't keep the irritation from her voice.

A thought suddenly occurred to Dooley. It seemed like a good thought, so he expressed it. "If you tell me yours, I'll tell you mine." It was something he'd heard on *General Hospital*, one of Gran's favorite soaps, though on the soap it had sounded different. More along the lines of 'If you show me yours, I'll show you mine.' The context had been a little fuzzy, and before they got down to business, Gran had turned off the TV. So he never did find out what it was exactly that this doctor and this nurse wanted to show to each other in that doctor's office. What meat they had on their sandwiches maybe. Or the type of sausage the doctor kept in his lunch box. Though it could have been a nice piece of cheese, of course.

Harriet blinked at him, even as Fifi and Rufus burst into raucous laughter.

"He's got you now, hasn't he, Harriet!" Rufus cried as tears rolled down his furry cheeks.

"Good thinking, Dooley," said Fifi, clapping him on the shoulder.

But Harriet wasn't laughing. She didn't even crack a smile. Instead she regarded him with barely concealed contempt. "That's what you get from associating with Max all these years," she snapped. "A filthy mind!"

And with these words, she strode off on a huff, leaving Dooley feeling bewildered and not a little concerned. Not only would he have to return to Max empty-pawed, but he would also have to inform him that his mind was filthy.

"I don't understand," he said finally. "Max is one of the cleanest cats I know. I'm sure his mind is as clean as the rest of him."

"Don't you worry about a thing, Dooley," said Rufus, speaking to him in fatherly tones. "Harriet might be upset now, but you know what she's like. She'll have completely forgotten about this in five minutes."

"A volcanic temper I think they call it," said Fifi.

"All I wanted to know was Harriet's secret," said Dooley. "Max wants to know, and Brutus wants to know, and Harriet isn't saying, so they sent me."

"Good thinking," said Fifi admiringly. "But then Max does have a big brain."

"Yeah, but it's dirty," said Dooley. "And I didn't even know. I don't think Max knows." And then he thought of something else. "How do you even clean a brain? It's inside your head, isn't it? Do you open up a person's head and take it out?"

"I'm sure it's not as bad as all that," said Fifi vaguely, exchanging a look with Rufus. "And now if you'll excuse us, Dooley, Rufus and I have work to do."

"You guys wouldn't know what Harriet's secret is, would you?"

"No, we wouldn't," said Fifi flatly. "We have no idea, do we, Rufus?"

"Absolutely not," said Rufus, but he was smiling, which gave the impression that he was giving a mixed message. Dooley didn't know what the mixed message was, but he did have the idea that these two might know more than they let on.

"It's just that Brutus is very worried, you know. He thinks that Harriet is having an affair with Kingman, because he saw the two of them together, and he also says he smelled Kingman in the rose bushes, which is their nooky nook, but now it's not their nooky nook anymore, since it's Kingman's nooky nook now. He's very upset, Brutus is. It's not nice when other cats go and do nooky in your nook."

He looked up when the two dogs started rolling about on the ground. At first he thought they were suffering from some kind of stomach ache, but then he saw they were actually laughing. He decided to leave them be. People were acting funny today. And when he said people he actually meant pets—dogs and cats both. Rolling on the ground. Being nice one minute and angry the next. Talking about dirty minds and nooky nooks and secret secrets. It was all very confusing.

CHAPTER 28

That night, cat choir was a subdued affair. Harriet wasn't talking to us, Brutus wasn't talking to Kingman, and Dooley kept babbling on about my mind needing a wash. Shanille, too, wasn't her usual self. The choir director usually comes to cat choir well-prepared, with a list of songs that she wants us to sing. But today she didn't seem to have made any preparations and said she wanted to wing it.

"Wing it?" I said. "What do you mean, wing it?"

"We'll simply start singing and see where it takes us," said Shanille in a breezy sort of way that was very unlike her.

"You can start without me," said Brutus, who was still quietly fuming.

"You're not singing tonight?" asked Shanille.

"No, I'm not. Not tonight and not any other night as long as Kingman is here."

"What do you mean?" asked Shanille.

"This town isn't big enough for the both of us," said Brutus. "So it's either Kingman or me."

But instead of getting upset, as I would have expected,

Shanille merely smiled. "That's fine, Brutus," she said. "Whatever you say."

Brutus frowned at her. "Didn't you hear what I said? I want you to choose, Shanille. Between me and Kingman."

"Of course," said Shanille. "Absolutely."

Brutus muttered something and stalked off, to go and fume some more under a nearby tree, from where he could keep an eye on Harriet and Kingman.

"He's concerned about Harriet," I explained. "He thinks she's having an affair with Kingman, and he's very unhappy about it."

"That's understandable," said Shanille, still continuing in that breezy way she had adopted. It was frankly infuriating.

"Do you have a secret, Shanille?" asked Dooley. "Because everybody else seems to have them. Max has a secret, and I have a secret, and Harriet has one, even though she refuses to tell us. And Brutus might have a secret, though I'm not sure."

"Oh, of course I have a secret," said Shanille.

"So what is it?"

"I can't tell you."

"But why?"

"Because the moment I tell you it's not a secret anymore, is it?"

Dooley thought about that for a moment. "But if you tell me, it will still be a secret to all the others, right? So technically it will still be a secret, only not to me."

Shanille smiled at Dooley's attempt at cunning. "Okay, you win, Dooley. I'll tell you guys my secret. But only if you promise not to tell anyone else, all right?"

"So what is it?" asked Dooley anxiously.

"I have a ninth nipple."

"A ninth nipple?"

"Yep, that's right. Wanna see?"

Dooley didn't seem particularly interested in Shanille's nipples, and neither was I, but she was already rolling on her back and counting out her nipples. In case you didn't know, cats have lots of nipples, usually six to eight. Some cats have more, others have less. Apparently Shanille's maker had gone the extra mile and had added a little bonus nipple. As secrets go, it wasn't exactly shocking, but Dooley and I went through the motions of expressing surprise, then admiration. Shanille seemed to think her ninth nipple was akin to Beethoven's Ninth Symphony, which I can tell you it most definitely was not.

"So what's your secret, Dooley?" asked Shanille when she had finished showing off her anomalous nipple.

Dooley, who hadn't been aware this was a contest, meekly told the story of his defecatory habit of despoiling Brutus's and Harriet's little love nook. It caused the choir conductor to crack a smile and then some. She turned to me. "And how about you, Max? Big cat like you must have a big secret, right?"

Dutifully I filled her in on my own habit of taking the first crack at a new bag of crispy kibble, but then Dooley said I had another secret to share, one Harriet had revealed to him. "Max has a dirty mind. Harriet says so. I don't know how it happened. Maybe some dirt got in through his nose or his ears. But now we've been racking our brains on how to wash his brains. Maybe Vena will know. I think we'll have to remove his brain from his head and wash it with strong soap."

Shanille produced a loud squeal of mirth at this surprise revelation, and before we knew what was happening, she'd gathered about a dozen cats around her, and was revealing my big secret! We could actually see how this mouth-to-mouth business worked and watch the news travel through the entire chowder of cat choir members. It was like watching wildfire spread through dry twigs.

"Dooley, my brain isn't dirty," I told my friend finally, when my so-called secret had done the rounds, and especially Dooley's solution of washing my brain with soap.

"But Harriet said so!"

"Harriet was just being mean, because you wouldn't tell her about Brutus's secret. So she lashed out, which is what she does when she doesn't get her way."

"So your brain isn't dirty?"

"My brain isn't dirty. In fact no brain can actually be dirty. Not literally, anyway." I didn't want to explain to him that a brain can be figuratively dirty, since that would only lead us astray. But at any rate, he was visibly relieved.

"Oh, Max, I was so worried about you! You have such a big, beautiful brain. It can't get dirty, cause then it would stop working. Like Odelia's car."

Odelia's pickup is an old jalopy that should have been put out to pasture a long time ago. But she's attached to the old thing, even though the engine keeps giving her grief. "My brain is fine," I said.

"What a relief! I'm so happy, Max!"

"Yeah, I'm happy, too," I said morosely. Not only had I been turned into the laughingstock of cat choir, but we still didn't know Harriet's big secret, and Brutus had now taken to whittling a piece of wood by cutting strips from it with his sharp claws, regarding Kingman malevolently all the while. I smelled trouble!

The big cat now came waddling up to us, a look of concern on his wide face. "What's gotten into Brutus?" he asked, discreetly directing an anxious look in the latter's direction. "He looks at me as if he wants to kill me!"

"Secrets and lies, Kingman," I said. "That's what this is all about, isn't it?"

"What are you talking about?" asked Hampton Cove's unofficial feline mayor.

"Brutus thinks you're having an affair with Harriet."

"An affair with Harriet! You have got to be kidding me!"

"No, I am not," I assured our voluminous friend. "So are you?"

"How can you ask me that, Max! Of course I'm not having an affair with Harriet!"

"You were seen canoodling."

"Canoodling!"

"Late at night."

"Late at night!"

"In the bushes."

"In the bushes!"

"Look, if you're going to repeat everything I say this is going to be a long night. Just tell me what's going on, Kingman. Because something is going on. I can feel it."

"In his brain," said Dooley helpfully. "In his very clean, not dirty at all, brain."

This caused Kingman to produce a high-pitched titter. But when he caught my stern look, he quickly simmered down. "Okay, I would tell you, but I can't."

"Of course you can."

"No, I can't. I was sworn to secrecy. And I may be a lot of things but I'm not a tattletale, Max," he added with a touch of pomposity.

"You're the exact definition of a tattletale, Kingman. I'll bet when people look up the word 'tattletale' in the dictionary your name is mentioned. So spill!"

But he clamped his lips together and shook his head emphatically.

"Fine," I said. "Be that way." Frankly I was getting a little fed up with this whole business. Which wasn't actually my business at all. Just something I got mixed up in. Well, me and the rest of Hampton Cove's cat population, apparently.

"Do you have secrets, Kingman?" asked Dooley.

"Oh, sure," said Kingman. "Plenty." He thought for a moment. "There's that time when I ate half the contents of the General Store meat locker, and Wilbur thought the store had been burgled so he called the police." He grinned at the recollection. "You should have seen his face when they checked the CCTV. I was grounded for a week after that stunt. And then of course I pooped in Wilbur's bed once. Or more than once, if I remember correctly."

"You pooped in Wilbur's bed?"

"He was involved with some devious female at the time. She used to kick me when Wilbur wasn't looking, and pinch me in the dark. The only way to get back at her was to leave a small deposit in the bed every time she stayed over. I think Wilbur finally got the message, cause he broke up with her soon after that."

I could have told him that the girlfriend had probably broken up with Wilbur after repeatedly finding poo in the bed and assuming Wilbur wasn't potty-trained.

"Okay, I guess that's all the secrets I've got for you today," said Kingman cheerfully. But then he caught Brutus's death-ray look amidships and gulped. "Max, can't you explain to Brutus I'm not having an affair with his girl. He looks ready to kill me!"

"I could tell him, Kingman—of course I could. But first I'd have to know this secret you're so anxious on keeping from us."

"I can't, Max! It's not my secret to tell! Harriet would kill me!"

I offered him a smile and a paw. He glanced down at the paw.

"Why are you shaking my paw, Max?" he asked.

"It's been a pleasure knowing you, Kingman. An honor."

"Gah," he grunted annoyedly, and waddled off on a huff.

"Is Kingman going to die, Max?" asked Dooley anxiously.

"I wouldn't be surprised, Dooley," I said. "I would not be surprised."

CHAPTER 29

Michele was in her room, prey to a sudden surge of melancholy. The realization that Isobel was gone had hit her suddenly after dinner, which they'd shared as a group, and she was still experiencing a powerful sense of loss.

She and Isobel hadn't been the best of friends, far from it, but she was still going to miss her. They'd shared so much over the years, both good and bad, and now all of a sudden that part of her life had ended in the tragic death of a woman who'd suffered as much or even more than Michele herself had.

Not many people lose their significant others in such a brutal fashion, and the loss of Dean and Gavin had hit them both hard. It had created a bond between them, a bond they had never acknowledged as such, but that was still there, as an invisible connection.

Isobel had borne the brunt of the tragedy, as her life had gradually spiraled out of control, ending in a quite humiliating brush with addiction, out of which she'd emerged, much to everyone's relief, only to plunge her family into turmoil once again with this autobiography nonsense.

Michele picked up her phone and waited for the call to connect. She was gratified to hear her mother-in-law's voice. The two women always had a good connection, and had only grown closer after Dean and Gavin had passed from their lives. "Hello, Marjorie," she said, much relieved. Her husband might be gone, and now Isobel, but she still had Bill and Marjorie, and her kids. "Yes, I'm fine. Yes, I'm hanging in there. No, we're not allowed to leave yet."

She glanced through the window, and imagined she could see the police car parked at the back gate. There was one positioned at the front of the house also. According to the detective in charge of the case both sentinels were there for their protection, just in case whoever killed Isobel might return. She thought the real reason was that the police thought someone in the house had killed Isobel, and until they knew who this person was, they weren't going to let them leave.

"How is Bill?" she asked. Bill might have passed the legal retirement age a while back but was still going strong, holding the reigns of his empire firmly in both hands. They all knew he was simply waiting for Michele's son Michael to take over. Michael wasn't ready yet, they also knew that. Running a large company like the Droba Group was a major challenge, and demanded a lot from a person. And even though Michael was doing well, acting as the group's vice-president and working directly under his grandfather's tutelage, it would be some time before he was at the point where he could take over and assume full control.

She talked to Marjorie for a few minutes, assuring her that everything was fine, and that the police had things well in hand and that she wasn't in any danger. She hung up and left the room, remembering suddenly that she needed to have a word with Berengária.

She found the woman in the kitchen, where she was checking the fridge and making a note about things she needed to buy. Berengária Morató was only a few years older than Michele, but looked about sixty. Her wizened features and gray hair tied back in a bun made her look much older than her years.

The housekeeper looked up when Michele entered. "We need to discuss dinner," she said. She'd totally forgotten about Berengária, what with the police sniffing around all day, and Isobel's murder.

"It not natural," said the woman, repeating a statement she'd made earlier that day. "You not stay here, in house where person dies. It bad karma."

"I know, Berengária, but what can we do? The police won't let us leave." At least they allowed the housekeeper to come and go. They could hardly suspect her of trying to murder them all in their beds.

"It very bad of them. They clean house."

"Yes, I know," said Michele, though she would have thought it was Berengária's job to clean the house, not the police.

"Clean energy," the woman clarified. "Remove evil spirit and sister ghost."

"Sister-in-law," she said, correcting a common misconception.

"They seal room, they clean," said Berengária with some vehemence.

"Yes, yes," she said, losing her patience. She didn't have time for a lot of superstitious claptrap. Not when she had a house full of worried people, who had to eat and sleep and live here together for who knows how much longer?

"Bad mojo," Berengária said, as if she hadn't made this point a hundred times before already. "Bad, bad mojo."

"Okay, so about lunch and dinner tomorrow. What did you have in mind?"

And as they set about discussing some of the practical arrangements that went into organizing a week like this, they quickly settled into the routine they'd come to rely on: Berengária wanted to know what Michele wanted to have for dinner, Michele made a suggestion, which Berengária immediately rejected out of hand, at which point she made a better suggestion, which Michele gratefully accepted. They went on like this for a while, checking the fridge and the larder until they had settled on tentative menus for lunch and dinner for the next few days, the cleaning schedule, laundry, flower arrangements—Michele insisted on having fresh flowers in all the rooms at all times—and finally the conversation returned to the topic that was on both their minds.

"Must be burglar," said Berengária with conviction. "Must be."

"The police were asking about that," said Michele as she leaned against the kitchen counter. God, she would murder for a glass of wine. But she knew that one glass led to a second, and she'd feel like hell in the morning. "Have there been a lot of burglaries in the neighborhood?"

"Oh, many, many," said the caretaker. "Dozens and dozens."

Michele thought she was probably exaggerating. If there really had been dozens of burglaries, the neighborhood would be a no-go zone, and the police would be patrolling the streets. "But if it was a burglary, why didn't they take anything from the other rooms?" she asked, voicing a question that was at the forefront of everyone's mind. "Why only Isobel's room? And why murder her?"

"These are bad people," said Berengária. "They love murder. It is what they do. Stealing and killing and maiming. They vicious killers. Evil *men*." She put the emphasis on the last word, and seemed ready to launch into her favorite subject: how evil men were. All men, no exception.

"Right," said Michele, pushing herself away from the counter. Conversations with Berengária were often frustrating for this exact reason: it was hard to get a sane word out of the woman, her mind filled with scary images and evil men everywhere she looked. Something in her past must have caused her to become this person, but frankly Michele didn't think she wanted to know.

CHAPTER 30

Ona had finished treating her face with the face cream Max had given her. She didn't know what was in it, but it made her skin glow with radiant health and removed all the impurities and remnants of the scars that had once burned red and angry. He really was a miracle worker. For a long time she thought this would be her life from now on: scarred and hurt and forced to be alone forever. And then Max had come along, and had lifted her out of the darkness and healed her life.

She was so grateful to him. Every day she said a silent prayer to this man, who had saved her from such a terrifying fate.

Joey and Zoey were lying at her feet, looking up at her with the kind of unconditional love and devotion only dogs are capable of. Odelia Poole had been there today with her two cats, and it wasn't that she didn't like cats, but there was simply no contest. Cats were wily animals, and you never knew what to expect. Dogs were loyal, and loving, and always happy to see you, whether you looked like the world's most beautiful woman, or the ugliest. They didn't care that your face had been damaged beyond repair—their love and devotion were unconditional.

She gave them a smile as she finished her bedtime routine by rubbing yet another cream into her face. And she was just checking a pimple on her temple when she caught movement from the corner of her eye. When she looked over, she saw to her horror that yet another envelope had been slipped under the door.

Immediately she rushed over and picked it up. Cutting a glance at the bathroom door, where Max was taking a shower, she ripped open the envelope and nervously extracted the small piece of paper, similar to the one she'd received that afternoon. The previous message had said, 'I know your secret!'

Which was bad enough, of course, but this one said: '$10.000 and I won't tell!'

She sank down on the bed. Ten thousand dollars or her secret was out. Her heart sank, and hot tears trickled down her cheeks.

At that moment, the bathroom door opened and Max strode out, wearing a dressing gown. She quickly wiped her tears, and hid the note behind her back, but too late.

"What's wrong?" he asked immediately. He took a seat next to her, and took the note. He read it and his expression hardened. "Who sent this?"

"I don't know," she said quietly. "Someone slipped it under the door just now."

"Must be someone in the house," he said. "There's no one else here." He frowned as he reread the note. "What do they mean? What aren't they going to tell?"

She looked down at her hands, lying on her lap, and didn't respond. She couldn't tell him. If she did, he'd leave her, she just knew he would.

"Ona, please," he said gently. "Just tell me."

"I-I can't," she said finally, and burst into tears for real this time.

He placed an arm around her and pulled her against his chest, rocking her gently while she cried.

"It's all right," he said. "Whatever it is, it's fine."

"No, it's not," she said miserably. "It's terrible."

"Oh, come on. It can't be as terrible as all that."

"Oh, Max," she said, turning a teary face up to him. "I did a horrible thing."

"Tell me," he urged kindly. "Let me be the judge of that. Please?"

She nodded, and started telling the story of the talent scout, the whole sordid tale emerging from her in starts and stops. He didn't respond at first, but finally, when she was done, he cupped her face between two large, warm hands, and said, gazing into her eyes, "That wasn't as bad as all that, now was it?"

"But it was. If people knew what I did—"

"So you took a meeting that was meant for your sister. It's not the end of the world. And besides, your sister did great, didn't she? She's an amazing doctor, who's helping lots and lots of people."

"But—"

"Look, if your sister had a powerful wish to become a model, she would have become a model, no matter what. As I see it, it wasn't a deep-seated wish, but more an idle young girl's dream. The way some kids want to become a fireman, or a policeman, or an astronaut. You, on the other hand, really wanted to become a model, and so you did. Your sister, once she grew out of this dream of being a model, fulfilled her real wish—her heart's desire—and became a doctor."

"You think?" she asked, hope surging in her bosom. All these years she'd thought of herself as some kind of villain. So maybe she wasn't so bad?

"Of course. Have you talked to Katey?"

She shook her head.

"Well, I think you should. I'm sure it'll be fine." He picked up the piece of paper. "And this person? I think you should tell the police. Cause chances are that whoever wrote this, killed Isobel Droba. I mean, how else did they know your secret unless they got it from Isobel's laptop, which the killer took, right?"

She hadn't thought of it that way. "You think I should tell the police?"

"Yes, I do. Is this the first note you got?"

"One arrived this afternoon." She got up and took the first note out of her purse and handed it to Max.

"Better if I don't handle it," he said. "I don't know for sure, but maybe the police can get a fingerprint off these notes, after taking your fingerprints for elimination purposes, of course."

She smiled for the first time. "You know an awful lot about this, Max."

"I watch a lot of crime shows," he said, returning her smile, then placing a gentle kiss on her lips.

She wrapped her arms around him and squeezed him tight. Her savior. "I'll tell the police tomorrow," she said. "And I'll talk to Katey. Just in case this blackmailer decides to go public with my big secret. I want Katey to hear it from me first."

"Good thinking," he said, burying his face in her hair. "God, you're beautiful."

She smiled. "Keep talking."

And so he did. And when one thing led to another, she finally forgot, for perhaps a few moments, the terrible events of that day, and felt happy again.

CHAPTER 31

Marge and Tex were in bed. Even though the day had been long and filled with the kinds of events that leave a person reeling, Marge wasn't feeling tired. Instead she felt sort of energized. She'd never been in this situation before, where the police thought she might actually have murdered someone. Well, apart from that time Chris Ackerman was murdered in her library, and for a short while she was the main suspect. This time there were many suspects, though, and as far as she could tell Chase hadn't yet decided which one of them might have done it.

Not that he had given them the benefit of his thoughts. Chase liked to play his cards close to his chest when working on a case, which was only to be expected. Even Odelia hadn't told her what was going on, just that they had one suspect under arrest, but she wasn't convinced he had something to do with the murder.

"How much longer do you think they'll keep us here?" she now asked.

"Not sure," said Tex. "But I don't mind, do you? Plenty of

food, company... And maybe tomorrow I'll finally manage to win a game for once."

Tex had lost another game that day. A singles game against Max Stinger. A loss that had stung even more than their loss against the Alemans that morning, for Stinger was a doctor, just like Tex, only a specialist, of course, a fact he didn't mind rubbing in from time to time. Clearly the old rivalry between family practitioners and specialists was still ongoing, with the latter feeling superior to the former.

"It's not right that we're still playing tennis," said Marge, "with Isobel lying dead in the morgue."

"What else can we do? They won't let us go home, so the best way to pass the time is to play tennis. It helps to keep people's mind off these terrible events."

Tex might have a point, of course, but Marge still found it disrespectful.

"Do you think we're suspects? Only Chase was acting so funny when I asked him about the case. He almost made me think they're suspecting us of all people."

"I'm sure Chase knows better than that. But he has a role to fulfill. He has to put on his cop cap, not his son-in-law cap when he's here talking to people."

It was odd seeing this side of Odelia's husband. He was so formal, so different. Odelia, bless her, was much the same as always. Though she couldn't tell them a lot either. Of course the investigation was still ongoing so there wasn't a lot to tell.

"It all seems to revolve around this book Isobel was writing, doesn't it?"

She looked up at this. "I thought it was a burglary?"

"Well, they took Isobel's phone and laptop, and left the rest of us undisturbed. So their thinking is that they were after Isobel's manuscript."

"How do you know? Did Chase tell you this?"

"No, some of the others did. Judging from Chase's line of questioning, that's the conclusion they seem to have reached. That it's all about that book of hers."

Marge was quiet for a moment, then said, "Do you have a secret, Tex? Are you in Isobel's book, you think?"

Tex cleared his throat. "I'm afraid so, honey. Yes, I think Isobel was getting ready to reveal my secret to the world."

"What secret would this be?" she asked, without looking up.

He swallowed audibly, then said, "I might as well tell you. It's going to come out sooner or later anyway." He heaved a deep sigh, while she braced herself. "You know how I've been saying I graduated from the Ross School Tennis Academy? And how I was trained by the great Pete Sampras himself? Well, I wasn't."

She smiled, much relieved. "That's your big secret? That Sampras didn't take you under his wing and teach you how to play tennis?"

"Yes, that's my big secret. Why, did you know already?"

"Of course I knew, honey! Everybody does!"

He was stunned, and stared at her for a good minute before stammering, "B-b-but why did nobody ever tell me!"

"Because they like you too much to cause you embarrassment."

"But I've been telling that story for years!"

"I know, and nobody has believed you for years."

"God," he said, dragging his fingers through his mane.

"So where did you learn how to play tennis, if it wasn't at that school?"

"The local YMCA," he said, which caused her to burst out laughing. He grinned. "They were cheap, and the coach was pretty good. Though not as good as Pete Sampras, obviously."

"Obviously."

"But he still taught me a couple of my signature moves." He demonstrated his backswing, almost clocking her on the nose. She would have told him that his 'signature moves' had never impressed anyone, but of course she didn't. After all they were amateurs, not professionals, and they were in it for their enjoyment, not to win the US Open.

They sat in companionable silence for a moment, then Marge said, "Shall I tell you my secret?"

"Please do."

And so she told him. And much to her satisfaction he hadn't known a thing about it, and it came as an absolute surprise to him. But he also seemed inordinately pleased, which warmed her heart all over again. He really was her dreamboat, wasn't he? He couldn't play tennis worth a damn, but he was grand.

CHAPTER 32

The day broke bright and glorious, and we found ourselves returning to the house where Isobel Droba had been murdered two nights ago now, for more interviews with potential suspects and a lot more sleuthing endeavors.

Even before we arrived, Ona Konpacka had phoned and asked to see us. She had a matter of some urgency to discuss with us, and for a brief moment Chase and Odelia were almost giddy with the hope that the model was going to confess to murder. Once we were in her room, where Ona sat regally on a highback chair and her boyfriend Max Stinger nervously paced about, it soon became clear that no confession was forthcoming. Instead she apprised Chase and Odelia of an attempt at blackmail that was in progress, handing them no less than three blackmail notes.

"This third one came this morning," she explained.

"'Once you're ready to make the transfer contact this number,'" Chase read.

"If I may ask, what's the secret?" asked Odelia, still hoping against hope that here sat their murderer.

"It's what I told you yesterday," said Ona. "About my sister and the talent scout?"

"Oh, right," said Odelia, and had a hard time keeping the disappointment from her voice. "So they want ten thousand not to tell that story, huh?"

"Yeah, it's not something I want people to know," said Ona. She was very quiet and looked uncomfortable about this whole blackmail business. "Though I told Max last night, and I'm going to tell my sister, which would take the wind of this blackmailer's sails."

"My advice would be to go through with the handing over of the money," Chase advised. "Once you've received instructions on where the rendezvous will be and when. Of course," he quickly added when Max Stinger started making protesting noises, "we'll be there every step of the way, so we can apprehend the culprit."

"You want to arrest the blackmailer?" asked Ona.

"Yes, of course."

"I think whoever is doing this killed Isobel," said Max.

"Oh, Max, don't say that," said Ona. "Now I'm thinking he might come after me next."

"No, but it stands to reason, doesn't it? First he steals the laptop, and when Isobel catches him he kills her, and now he's using the information he got from that laptop to blackmail people."

Chase looked up sharply. "You think there's more than one victim, sir?"

The doctor shrugged. "I don't know. But if he's blackmailing Ona, there's bound to be others, wouldn't you say?"

"Max?" said Ona.

"Yes," I said, even as the other Max turned to his girlfriend.

Dooley laughed. "That's funny. You've got a soulmate, Max."

"A namesake, more like," I said.

"What do you think?" asked Ona.

"I think this is a good idea," I said.

"I'm not sure about this," said the other Max.

"It's up to you, of course, Miss Konpacka," said Chase. "But if we want to catch this person, this is the best way to go about it."

"You won't be in any danger," Odelia assured the model. "We'll be close by, keeping an eye out for this person, and we'll nab him the moment he shows his face."

Max finally nodded his agreement, even though he still seemed reluctant.

Ona took a deep breath. "All right," she said. "I'll do it."

"Great," said Chase.

A knock sounded at the door, and we all jumped. But when Odelia went to open it, it wasn't the blackmailer but Vena Aleman.

"I heard you had arrived," she explained. "Could I have a word with you?"

"Of course," said Odelia.

And as we left the room, Chase stayed on to explain to Ona how they were going to organize this sting operation. He also asked if he could take a look at her shoes. Judging from the look on Max Stinger's face, he seemed to think Chase was some kind of shoe fetishist, but Chase quickly dissuaded him from this notion.

※

The room where Vena and Glenn Aleman were staying looked just about the same as Ona's room, with the minor difference that they didn't have the nice view of the tennis courts the model and her surgeon boyfriend had. Instead they looked out across the neighbor's backyard, who owned a pool which was filled with screaming and splashing children.

Glenn wasn't present for the interview, and I wondered what Vena was going to tell us. Dooley had his own ideas, of course.

"I think she did it, Max. I think she murdered Isobel!"

"Why on earth would Vena murder Isobel?"

"Because that's the kind of person she is! Always prodding us with needles, poking us with sharp instruments, cutting us open to look inside our bellies. She's a murderous maniac, Max, we all know that. And now she's finally taken it too far. She's gone and murdered a human. And we all know humans don't mind when pets are being murdered, but they scream bloody murder when another human is killed."

There was some logic to what he was saying, of course. Humans seem mainly concerned about their fellow humans being killed, not so much when members of other species suffer the same fate. Though I couldn't believe Vena would take the innate murderous instinct that all veterinarians seem to share to this level.

"I know that Isobel was writing that horrible book of hers," said Vena, who had taken a seat on a chair near the window, with Odelia pulling up a second chair. The vet's demeanor was a far cry from her customary bluff and hearty way. Instead she looked pale and drawn, and she sat slumped in her seat, head bowed. "And now that she's dead, and her laptop has been stolen, all the secrets are bound to come out sooner or later. So I'd rather you heard it from me than someone else." She took a deep, shuddering breath. "I once killed a patient."

"See!" Dooley cried triumphantly. "I told you!"

"Shush, Dooley," I said. "Let's hear what she has to say."

"It was a long time ago," said Vena. "I was just starting out, fresh from vet school, and I must have made a mistake in the dosage of the sedative I was administering. The animal—Freddie, it was called—died, and I was forced to own up to my mistake to the owners. Lucky for me they were very understanding, and didn't file a complaint. Also, Freddie was old and on its last legs at that point, and wouldn't have lived much longer anyway. So maybe what I did was an act of mercy, even though it was an accident."

"What type of animal was it?" asked Odelia.

"A gerbil," said Vena. Her cheeks were flushed, and she looked shamefaced. "I never told anyone, except Glenn, of course. And Isobel. I don't know why I told her. It came up in conversation once, and she was so easy to talk to, you know. There was something comforting about her, something kind and wonderful, that made you want to confide in her, and tell her all your secrets. She always said she should have been a pastor." She smiled a wistful smile. "At least if she was a pastor, she would have been bound by the seal of confession. Now she was free to write about it in her book. Which will cause quite a stir once its secrets are revealed."

"You don't know if that will happen," said Odelia. "Did you... Did you by any chance receive a blackmail letter, Vena?"

Vena shook her head. "No, I didn't. Why, is the killer blackmailing people now?"

"I'm not sure," said Odelia evasively.

"God. If the truth comes out, I'll be ruined. Who's going to trust me now? They'll think I'm bound to kill their precious pets."

Odelia squeezed the vet's arm. "I trust you, Vena, and I'm sure a lot of people know what a great veterinarian you are and won't abandon you either."

"She should abandon her," Dooley grumbled. "If I'd known she was in the habit of murdering her patients, I would never have agreed to be treated by her."

"Whether you agree or not, Dooley, makes no difference at all," I said somberly.

"That's true," said Dooley. We shared a look of dismay. It's one thing to suspect that your vet is secretly a murderous butcher, but another to hear it from her own lips. As I saw it we'd had a lucky escape so far. We could have been that gerbil. We all could have been that gerbil!

"Poor Freddie," said Dooley.

"Poor us," I said.

"Could I see your shoes for a moment, Vena?" asked Odelia now.

"Sure," said Vena, getting up. "What's this about?"

"Oh, just a routine check," said Odelia cheerfully.

"Better check her luggage for dead gerbils!" Dooley yelled as the two women disappeared into the next room. "Remember Freddie!"

CHAPTER 33

Perlita felt utterly embarrassed as she watched Detective Kingsley go through her collection of shoes. "I'm sorry about yesterday," she said. "For making such a spectacle of myself."

"That's all right, Mrs. Gruner," said the detective as he picked up her pair of high heels and closely examined the heels. "What size would you say these are?"

Michele had given Perlita a new room and now she was officially separated from Nathan—at least for the duration of this retreat, which was already turning into a nightmare. She had no idea what she'd do once they were home again.

She felt betrayed, both by Izzy and her husband. But since she was also cheating on him, she could hardly blame him for what he'd done. They were in the same boat, after all. Already she'd called Izzy, to cancel the exhibition, and to tell her they were through, and Izzy had told her that Nathan had done the exact same thing, and said to find another agent.

The young artist had sounded miserable. Clearly this was the worst day of her life: she just lost the exhibition which was going to launch her career and her agent both on the same day. Perlita almost felt sorry for the girl. But then she considered how she'd been using them for their connections, and to further her career, and every trace of compassion vanished. She was a calculating little minx who'd taken a gamble and lost. And now she'd have to suffer the consequences. Just like they all did.

Nate had reached out to her that morning, calling her and sending messages and knocking on her door, but she'd ignored him. She didn't want to see him or talk to him. And she most definitely did not want to discuss the affair. Or affairs, plural.

"Done," said Detective Kingsley finally, and got up.

"So have you found the murderer?" she asked. "Only Michele told me you made an arrest? Her niece's boyfriend?"

"Mr. Rocamora is a person of interest, but at this moment he is not under arrest," said the cop, sounding very formal. He then regarded her closely. "You haven't by any chance received a blackmail letter, have you, Mrs. Gruner?"

"No, I haven't. Why, is there a blackmailer active?"

"I couldn't say," said the cop carefully, then thanked her for her cooperation.

"So how long do you think we'll have to stay in this place? Only after what happened between me and Nate, things are a little strained at the moment."

The police detective was very kind. He told her that he understood how difficult it was for her to have to stay under the same roof with the man she was now estranged from. And no, he couldn't say how long this situation would go on.

He left, then, and she walked over to the window. Out on the court, she could see Nate playing a game against Glenn Aleman. Apparently he wasn't too bowled over by their separation. He was even laughing, the traitorous bastard.

Chase had checked Ona's shoes, and also Perlita's, Michele's and even his mother-in-law's modest collection of footwear. He hadn't found a single pair of stiletto heels, and definitely not the murder weapon they were looking for. As far as shoe size was concerned, there wasn't a lot of difference between the ladies. And if Odelia didn't forget to check Vena's shoes, they'd have covered all the women present. He'd also used the opportunity to take a closer look at their faces, but he couldn't imagine any of them having gone through life as Gavin Droba. Their features simply did not match the picture of Gavin he carried in his pocket.

The man had had a wide face, with a flattened nose, and pockmarked skin. He was also short and chunky, and even though a person can change their face, it's probably hard to make yourself taller by several inches.

He sighed. This investigation wasn't going the way he had hoped. So far they had nothing. Now if only he could prove that this detective who'd been tailing Rocamora was in on the whole business, but by all accounts Mark Devine had an impeccable record. Respected by his colleagues and his employers, there wasn't anything in his file to suggest he might collude with a murderer.

His phone chimed and he took it out of his pocket. "Kingsley," he said curtly.

"Yes, hi, detective," spoke a voice he vaguely recognized. "Alison Droba. I was wondering when I can have my car back? Your people took it, and I need it."

"I'll check with the forensics team," he said curtly. "Anything else?"

"Yes, I thought you might be interested to know that the detective I hired to find my father called me just now. He found him, though not in Mexico but in Belize. Turns out he'd been living there all this time, under an assumed name, which is why it took so long to find him. He owned a bar."

"A bar?"

"Yes. A far cry from managing a multinational corporation, wouldn't you say?"

"Are you going to reach out to him?"

"I would, only it turns out he died three years ago."

"He…"

"Yes, died and was buried under his assumed name. Sebastian Dixon."

"How did he die, if I may ask?"

"He was hit by a car and died."

Chase could hear that she was upset, and even though she was still a suspect, he softened. He wasn't a hard-hearted man, quite the contrary. "My sincerest condolences, Miss Droba."

"Oh, you know," she said in a shaky voice. "It's been seven years. I was quite young when he left, so it's not as if I…" Her voice broke. "I'm sorry, detective."

"No, that's all right. It's understandable that you would feel this way. Even though he left you and your mother, he was still your dad."

"Yeah, he was," she said quietly. "And now I don't have any parents left."

"Did your mother know, you think? About your dad, and the fact that he died?"

"I'm not sure. She might have known. Maybe that's why she acted so cold when I told her I'd hired someone to find him. It didn't occur to me before, but she could have hired a detective herself, and found out what happened. But if she did she never told me about it."

"If she did, it will be in her book, I imagine," said Chase.

"Yeah, that stupid book of hers," said Alison. "The book that got her killed."

Chase didn't respond. Odelia might think that Isobel's murder was connected to the book she was writing, and so might everyone else, but he still thought this whole case revolved around Jason Rocamora and the lovely but very deceptive Miss Droba. "By the way, Alison, what size shoe would you say you have?"

"Just get me back my car," Alison snapped, and promptly hung up.

CHAPTER 34

Even though Mark Devine wasn't the PI Alison had hired to find her dad, he worked for the same detective agency, and since his colleague Steve Martin was still in Belize, where he'd been instrumental in finding the missing man, it was up to Mr. Devine to fill us in on the details of Mr. Martin's successful investigation.

The detective had agreed to meet in front of the house, and so we found ourselves piling into his modest metallic gray Renault Clio which was probably parked in the same spot where it had been parked on the night of the murder.

Chase had ordered a background check on the detective, but so far he'd come out squeaky clean, much to the cop's disappointment. Chase's line of inquiry was that Mark Devine was somehow in collusion with Alison and her criminal fiancé, but so far the evidence didn't bear out that theory.

Which was perhaps the reason Chase wasn't as friendly to his colleague as he could have been.

Mark Devine seemed surprised when Chase was accompanied not only by Odelia, introduced as a civilian consultant, but also by Odelia's two cats. We weren't introduced as such, though the term feline consultant would have been appropriate. But Uncle Alec, when he appointed his niece, hadn't extended the courtesy to Dooley and myself, unfortunately. As it was, we were simply part of the decoration, one could say. The wallpaper, perhaps. Or background noise.

"So you found Gavin Droba, did you?" asked Chase tersely.

"Well, not me personally, no," said Mr. Devine, who was a slovenly dressed individual in his early fifties with a distinct stubble on his chin and haphazardly arranged strands of gray hair covering a wide dome that was fast going bald. "But yeah, we found Droba, who had adopted the name Sebastian Dixon for his purposes. We found him living in Corozal, a small town eighty-four miles north of Belize City. Took us a long time to find him, too. He hadn't made things easy."

"He was operating a bar?"

"A chain of restaurants, actually. The man had done well for himself. Also owned several pieces of real estate property. So he must have had some capital when he arrived, so he could set himself up in business over there. Which suggests he didn't leave the country empty-handed but with a cache of capital so he could start over. As the son of Bill Droba, tire king, he was of course the heir to a considerable fortune, so he must have squirreled away a nest egg he could use for a rainy day. Only that rainy day came a lot sooner than he thought when he accidentally killed his brother and had to flee the country."

"He died?"

"Yeah, he did," said the detective, patting his wavy strands of hair. "Three years ago. Car mounted the sidewalk and scooped him up. He died on impact."

"Was it an accident, you think?"

The detective shrugged. "According to the police report it

was. Driver was drunk. Witnesses said he was slaloming across the road. After he ran down Droba he rammed a convenience store and injured several customers. So yeah, looks like it was an accident—nothing to suggest it wasn't."

"Sad ending for Mr. Droba," said Odelia.

"Yeah, you can say that again," the PI confirmed. "Oh, there's one other thing I wanted to tell you. When Dean Droba was killed, there was a persistent rumor going around that the Droba Group was in some kind of financial trouble. Financial malfeasance, actually."

"Which would have been Gavin's domain," said Chase. "Since he was CFO."

"Yeah, that's right. Bill Droba had handed control of the group to his sons, but apparently the brothers weren't handling things as well as could be expected, and at the time of Dean's death, the vultures were circling, and there were rumors of a hostile takeover being in the works by one of their Italian competitors."

"So what happened?"

"Well, Dean died, and as luck would have it, a sizable sum had been settled on him by way of life insurance. We're talking millions here. The insurance eventually paid out and the company was saved by the skin of their teeth. The money tied them over a rough patch, and once Bill took over it was smooth sailing again." He grimaced. "You could say that Dean dying was a blessing in disguise. A couple of months longer and the Droba Group would have been no more."

"Is Bill still running the group?" asked Chase, jotting down a few notes.

"Yeah, but not for much longer. Bill is pushing seventy, and he's been grooming his grandson Michael to take over."

"So they're skipping a generation."

"Yeah, out of necessity. With Dean dead and Gavin gone,

Bill had no choice but to step in. And Michele and Isobel, the widows, had no interest in the business."

"But Michael has?"

"Oh, yeah. By all accounts he's some kind of business wunderkind."

"Michael is Michele's son?" asked Odelia.

"Yeah, he is. He has a sister, Drew, but she's not involved in the business. She's an anthropologist. She's in Mexico right now, actually, on some dig down there." He rubbed his face. "I still haven't told Bill about what happened to his son."

"Isn't that Alison's job?" asked Chase.

"Yeah, I know, but the least I can do is tell him personally. But I couldn't get him on the phone. As you know I told Alison, who took the news pretty bad. I'm assuming Bill will want the body brought back here, to have him buried in the family plot." He glanced over to Chase. "So have you caught Isobel's killer yet?"

"Not yet," said Chase. "But we're close." He tapped his notebook. "We might make an arrest today."

"Alison told me you arrested her boyfriend?"

"We released him," said Chase somberly.

"Poor kid," said the detective. "First her mom died, and now she finds out her dad died, too. She's got no one left to walk her down that aisle when she ties the knot." He held up his hand and shook Chase's, then reached back and shook Odelia's. He came close to shaking my paw, but drew the line there. "Well, if there's anything else you need to know, you've got my number."

"Yeah, I've got your number, all right," said Chase, and we got out. As the detective drove off in a cloud of petrol fumes, he added, "He's still a suspect."

Stubborn to the last.

CHAPTER 35

The trap for the blackmailer had been set, and the location the dastardly fiend had chosen was our local park, coincidentally also the place where cat choir likes to convene at night. Ona Konpacka had sent a message to the blackmailer that she was prepared to pay the demanded sum of ten thousand smackeroos, and the blackmailer had immediately replied with a time and a place for the drop-off.

The phone number itself wasn't registered. It was a so-called burner phone, with a prepaid SIM card that couldn't be traced or connected to a single person. It was still the way criminals covered their tracks, even though lately encrypted phones had become quite the rage. But clearly our blackmailer wasn't as sophisticated as all that.

And so we were relegated, not for the first time, to the bushes, which were located near the trash can conveniently placed next to a park bench. No one was sitting on the park bench at the moment, and apart from Ona, who had deposited the envelope containing the money into the trash can, all was quiet.

"What is taking them so long?" Chase grumbled, checking his watch.

"They're careful, making sure they're not walking into a trap," said Odelia.

She and Chase had placed a plastic bag on the ground, on which they were now seated, and neither of them looked very comfortable. Then Dooley and I had a better deal: cats are used to sitting in bushes watching the world go by. Our tushes are perfectly shaped for this type of situation. And even though it's usually birds we like to watch, or the odd mouse or critter, this time we were on the lookout for much bigger prey. An actual blackmailer and possible murderer!

Chase was hoping that when we nabbed Ona's blackmailer, we'd also catch Isobel Droba's killer. And I guess he had reason for this optimism: how else had the blackmailer gotten hold of Ona's big secret? They must have grabbed the laptop after ending Isobel's life in such a brutal fashion.

"Odd that Michele's daughter would be in Mexico right now," Chase mused. "Just when they've discovered the whereabouts of her uncle Gavin."

"Nothing odd about that," said Odelia. "She's an anthropologist, so she goes where the work is. I wouldn't read too much into that. Just a coincidence, that's all."

"I don't like coincidences," said Chase. "What if they're all in on it? The whole family? They killed Dean, so they could get that insurance money and save the company, and then they killed Gavin, just in case he opened his mouth and revealed the truth."

"Gavin's death was an accident, Chase. You heard what that detective said."

"Mh," said Chase, telling us exactly what he thought of Mark Devine.

"Look," said Odelia. "Isn't that Michele's housekeeper?"

A slim lady approached the park bench. She had a

wizened face and gray hair tied back in a bun in a way that looked painful. She had a furtive way about her, looking left and right. At first she walked straight past the bench, halted after thirty yards, then doubled back. And as she did, she glanced down into the trash can, and quick as a flash grabbed the envelope and hurried off.

"Not so fast!" Chase boomed as he rocketed out of his hiding place.

The woman, who clearly wasn't as old as she looked, paused for a moment, staring at Chase as if he was the boogeyman, then whirled around and started running in the opposite direction.

Chase, cursing under his breath, took off in pursuit, as did Odelia.

Dooley and I would have followed them, but frankly I didn't see the point. If Chase, a trained sportsman and cop, couldn't catch her, or Odelia, who also enjoyed spending time in the gym, no one could. And besides, I believe in conserving one's energy. You never know when you might need it.

"What's the name of that woman?" asked Dooley as we watched the trio disappear in the distance.

"Berengária Morató," I said. "She works for Michele as a housekeeper."

"So maybe Michele is the blackmailer, and this Berengária is doing her bidding?"

"We'll know soon enough," I said, as I watched the trio running back in our direction. Sooner or later, if you wait long enough, everything comes back. Like leg warmers, you know, or ABBA. And so Berengária Morató was now running up to us, though she was also running out of steam, I could tell. The moment she drew level with us, I stepped forward, and the housekeeper tripped and fell.

Look, did I feel good about tripping up this woman? No, I

did not. But she was a blackmailer, so there are mitigating circumstances for what I did.

Chase was quick to apprehend the suspect, and Odelia, when she finally caught up with us, panting and sweating profusely, lamented that she was out of practice. Of course she had a perfect excuse, having pushed a large infant out of her stomach in the recent past. She rested her hands on her knees to catch her breath, while Chase placed a nice pair of shiny cuffs on the housekeeper's wrists, and informed her that she was under arrest.

The woman was muttering some words in a language that I couldn't understand. They didn't sound very nice, though, and were mainly directed at Chase, whom she seemed to have taken an instant dislike to. A cop's fate, I guess.

Chase didn't seem to mind. In fact he looked over the moon. He'd finally nabbed his man, even though she was a woman, and in due course the lady was put in a squad car and carted off to the precinct for processing and questioning.

CHAPTER 36

Once more we found ourselves on the outside looking in. In this case we were in the viewing room, looking into the interview room, where Chase was interrogating his suspect. Berengária wasn't playing ball, though. She was refusing to explain what she was doing in the park, and why she was targeting Ona. But they'd found the phone on her that the blackmailer used, and when a search of her apartment was conducted, they'd found several more blackmailing notes she had carefully prepared, as well as a list of the people she was targeting.

It was an interesting list, and featured Michele Droba, Vena Aleman, Nathan Gruner, Perlita Gruner and... Marge Poole!

What the search hadn't produced was Isobel's laptop, wallet or phone. And since Miss Morató wasn't talking, there was no evidence to suggest that she was Isobel's killer. But clearly she was in possession of the manuscript, and the secrets it contained—a gold mine for a cunning blackmailer.

Chase soon gave up, especially when Berengária demanded a lawyer be present for the interview, and the lady was arrested on the grounds of the evidence they had discovered: the blackmail.

We returned to the house, where Odelia went in search of her mother, to ask her about the blackmail. Finding Marge's name on Berengária's list had obviously greatly concerned her. She found her mom at the tennis court, where she was watching a game between Tex and Glenn Aleman. Tex was losing, I guess, for he didn't look happy, while the bookstore owner was grinning from ear to ear.

Odelia took a seat on the bench next to her mom. Marge looked up and smiled. "Hey, honey. I wasn't expecting to see you here. How is the investigation going?"

"Chase just made an arrest," said Odelia. "Berengária Morató was arrested on charges of blackmail."

"Berengária? But she's Michele's housekeeper."

"I know. She's also a blackmailer." She eyed her mom closely. "Mom, is there something you want to tell me? Only, your name was on Berengária's list of targets."

Marge swallowed uncomfortably. "Honey, I don't know what to say."

"Did you receive a blackmail note, Mom? Or did Dad?"

"No, we haven't received anything."

"Which means she must have targeted Ona first," said Odelia thoughtfully, "and was waiting to target the others until she was sure she could pull it off."

"Marge has a secret, Max," said Dooley. "I can see it in her eyes. She looks guilty."

"She does look guilty, doesn't she?" I said.

"She's a bad liar, Max. Some people are good liars, but she's lousy at it."

Marge must have overheard us, for she turned to me and said, "You shouldn't be so quick to judge, Dooley. I have a perfectly good reason to keep my private affairs private."

"Which is?" I asked, curious now.

But Marge closed her lips and turned away, clearly not prepared to talk.

"Mom, you have to tell me what's going on," said Odelia. "This has gone beyond you and Dad's private lives. We're in the middle of a murder investigation here."

"This has got nothing to do with your investigation," said Marge. "Trust me."

"I would, but if you don't tell me, Chase will have to bring you in for questioning. You and Dad."

Marge shook her head. "I guess that's what you get when your daughter marries a cop. Your private life isn't your own anymore. Everything becomes everybody's business."

"Why, is it so bad?" asked Odelia quietly, as she touched her mom's arm.

Marge persisted for a moment, then finally relented. "Okay, fine. If you have to know, I once published a series of short novels under a *nom the plume*." She squeezed her eyes closed. "The name I used was Kitty Velvet, and the stories were of an erotic nature."

For a moment, no one spoke, as we digested this revelation. Then Dooley burst into laughter, quickly followed by myself, and even Odelia had a hard time keeping a straight face.

Marge glared at her daughter. "It's not funny. If word spread about this I'd be the laughingstock of the whole town. People would read the stories and quote them back to me. I have a lot of loyal readers at the library, and they'd have a field day if they knew I once attempted to be a writer."

"But Mom!" said Odelia. "This is wonderful. I didn't know you were a writer."

"I'm not," said Marge, carefully studying her fingernails. "I only sold a handful of copies, and my reviews were pretty damning. Which is why I don't want anyone to know about this. I have a reputation to uphold, you know." She looked anxious all of a sudden. "You won't tell anyone, will you? I don't want people to know."

"I won't," Odelia promised. "This has no bearing on the case whatsoever, and I'm sure Chase will agree, and Uncle Alec."

"God, you'll have to tell Chase, I guess, and my brother. And before you know it, word will spread and I'll have to leave town and go and live on the other side of the country. Or Scotland."

"Why Scotland?"

Marge shrugged. "I've always wanted to go, just never had the chance."

"You won't have to move to the other side of the country or Scotland, Mom," Odelia assured her mother. She seemed inordinately pleased with this secret. Which was understandable. She had probably thought the worst, and being responsible for the penning of a few erotic novels didn't exactly constitute a crime. A crime against literature, maybe, if the novels were that bad, but not punishable by law. "So Kitty Velvet, huh?" she said, grinning widely. "I like the name, Mom. Very saucy."

"Huh. You're funny," Marge said, clearly not happy with this denouement.

"So what kind of novels are they?"

"Remember those *Fifty Shades of Grey* books? Well, something like that. Only in my novels he wasn't called Mr. Grey but Mr. Black."

"Very original."

"I never said the novels were good. In fact they're probably pretty bad."

"I'll read them and I'll give you my personal review," said Odelia.

Marge puckered up her brow in despair. "Oh, please don't!"

"But I have to. My mom is a writer, so I have to read them."

"God, what have I done?" said Marge, shaking her head.

"I'm sure they're not as bad as all that. I bet they're great."

"No, they're not."

Odelia was smiling before herself for a moment, then launched into her second inquiry which might be deemed embarrassing. "So what's Dad's secret?"

"That's easy. You know how your dad always claims he was trained by Pete Sampras?"

"He wasn't?"

Marge shook her head. "He never met Mr. Sampras in his life. He also didn't go to that posh tennis school he's always talking about. Instead he took a couple of lessons at the YMCA. Which probably explains why he's such a terrible player."

Tex had struck out again, and Glenn was pumping his fist in a victory sign. "Yesss!" the bookstore owner shouted, much to Tex's dismay. But he showed himself a graceful loser, for he shook Glenn's hand before stepping off the court.

"I told Odelia about Pete Sampras," said Marge.

"Oh?" said Tex.

"I had to. They arrested Berengária, who was going to blackmail us."

"She was, was she?" said Tex as he drew a towel across his face and neck.

"Your name wasn't on her list, though," said Odelia. "So looks like you were in the clear."

"I wasn't on the blackmailer's list?" asked Tex, looking disappointed. "But why?"

"I guess your secret wasn't big enough, honey," said Marge.

Tex's lips formed a perfect O, and we all laughed, even Marge. Or should I say Kitty Velvet?

"I want to read Marge's stories about Mr. Black, too, Max," said Dooley. "I think she is a much better writer than she's letting on. I'm very proud of her. And maybe we can even start a reading club. I'm sure Harriet will be excited about reading Marge's books, too, and maybe Shanille and all the others."

Alarmed, I looked up at Odelia, who had also heard my friend's words. I shared a look of understanding with my human, and somehow I had the feeling those Kitty Velvet books would soon be a thing of the past. I don't know how, but I was quite sure they'd disappear into the mists of time, never to be seen again.

CHAPTER 37

We were in Uncle Alec's office, where the Chief had summoned his detective and his niece to give him an update on the case. The Drobas were a prominent family with a lot of clout, and the death of Isobel had reverberated throughout the community and was receiving plenty of attention in the media. And since nobody likes bad publicity, the town council was putting pressure on the mayor to put pressure on the chief of police to find Isobel's killer and put the case to bed—fast!

And so now Uncle Alec was putting pressure on Chase and Odelia.

"I still think Jason is our guy," Chase insisted. "Him and Alison both."

"But he can't be," said Odelia. "Mark Devine swears Alison never left the car."

"He's lying. No detective engaged in a stakeout keeps his eye on his target all the time. He closes his eyes for a nap, or he reads something on his phone, or orders a pizza and has to pay the delivery guy, or he steps out of the car for a pee."

"Don't private detectives pee in bottles?" asked Uncle Alec.

"Look, I don't care. I'm sure he lost sight of Alison at some point, and that's when she and the boyfriend crawled up to Isobel's room and killed her. There's no other explanation."

"So what about this blackmailer?" asked the Chief. "This Morató woman?"

"Possible," Chase allowed. "But she's not talking. And we searched her apartment and found no trace of Isobel's things, or the murder weapon."

"You didn't find anything on Rocamora either," the Chief pointed out.

"Yeah, I know," Chase sighed, finger-combing his shaggy mane.

"So all you've got so far is circumstantial evidence. Nothing concrete."

Both Chase and Odelia gave the chief of police a sheepish look.

"So what about these stiletto heels? You searched all the rooms?"

"We did. But so far we haven't found them. Or the murder weapon."

"Okay, so what about your theory that somehow Gavin Droba is involved? That he had a sex change operation and is one of the guests of his sister-in-law?"

"Gavin Droba died three years ago, Chief, so that's a dead end, I'm afraid."

The Chief slammed the desk with a meaty fist, causing us all to jump. "I don't believe this. You've arrested two people, looked at a dozen others, and so far you've got absolutely nothing to show for it? I want results, people, results! And I want them yesterday! I've got the mayor breathing down my neck—"

"That's not such a hardship, is it, Chief?" said Chase with a grin. But his boss wasn't having it.

"Look, just get me Isobel's killer, will you?" He was eyeing his niece when he said this. "Don't make me regret putting you on this case, Odelia. I get enough flak as it is for adding a civilian to my team. Don't prove the naysayers right."

"I won't, Uncle Alec," said Odelia. "I promise."

"Don't make promises you can't keep, honey," he warned.

She put on a brave face. "We'll get Isobel's killer." She glanced down at me.

"And don't look at your damn cat!" Uncle Alec cried. "Since when is a cat in charge of a murder inquiry in my town? It's unnatural! Not to mention illegal! If people found out…" He shook his grizzled head. "Just catch me that killer. Before I lose the rest of my hair."

❦

"Uncle Alec didn't seem very happy, did he, Max?" said Dooley.

"No, he most certainly did not," I agreed.

"Why is it illegal for a cat to run a murder inquiry, Max?"

"Probably because we don't have the necessary credentials."

"What credentials?"

"Well, we didn't go to the police academy, did we? We didn't get the badge."

"I didn't even know cats could go to the police academy."

"We can't. Police academy is for humans only."

"Too bad. I bet we'd make excellent recruits."

It was unorthodox, of course, for a cat to assist in a murder inquiry, but from my point of view I was simply trying to help. And if Uncle Alec didn't appreciate my assistance, I could always abandon my post and leave things as they were.

But once we were back in the car it became apparent that my assistance was still very much appreciated, for Odelia turned to me and asked, "Any ideas, Max? Anything we're missing?"

"It's Rocamora, isn't it?" said Chase. "Somehow he's bamboozling us."

"Frankly I have no idea," I said. "At this point it could be anyone, as far as I can tell. It could be Jason Rocamora, it could be Berengária Morató, or it could be some unknown burglar who just happened to pick Isobel's room to burgle that night, and Isobel was in the wrong place at the wrong time." Though the fact that the killer had carried out such a frenzied attack with a stiletto heel seemed to contradict that particular possibility. That attack seemed personal to me. And also, a house-to-house hadn't revealed anything suggesting an active burglar.

"We need to have another crack at the Morató woman," said Chase. "Though now that she's lawyering up, she's unlikely to give us anything."

"She's obviously read Isobel's manuscript," said Odelia.

"Which suggests she's the one who took the laptop."

And as we all chewed on the different possibilities, I wondered about the people still locked up in the house. Maybe it was time to let them go now.

CHAPTER 38

The arrest of Berengária had thrown Michele's perfectly ordered life out of whack, or at least the parts of her life that the murder of Isobel hadn't upended. She still had a house full of guests, who needed to be fed, and she had no idea how to go about it. So when Marge and Vena offered to help prepare dinner, she gratefully accepted. The ladies descended on the kitchen, and started looking through cupboards and checking the fridge preparatory to deciding what to cook for dinner.

"I heard the police discovered that Gavin died," said Marge as she stood chopping onions, while Michele sniffed from a container filled with a viscous red substance. "I'm so sorry for your loss, Michele."

"Thanks," said Michele warmly, appreciating her friend's kind words. "It wasn't the police who found Gavin, though, but a private investigator my niece Alison hired." Alison had always been anxious to find her dad, and now that she had finally succeeded, hopefully she would find some peace knowing he died happy. Or at least successful, operating a chain of restaurants in Belize, of all places.

"You know, I was thinking that maybe your sister-in-law was right after all," said Vena, engaged in washing and picking apart a head of lettuce in the sink. "Maybe secrets are corrosive, and should be brought out into the open. I mean, I told some people about my biggest secret today, and it wasn't as bad as I thought."

"What is your big secret, Vena, if I may ask?" said Marge.

"I once accidentally killed a gerbil," said Vena. She proceeded to explain the circumstances of the death of this gerbil named Freddie, and Michele had to admit the revelation wasn't as terrible as Vena had clearly feared. "I carried that secret around with me for years. Afraid it would come out."

"I once wrote a series of short erotic novels," Marge blurted out. "I told my daughter today, and my husband last night, and I have to say they took the news well."

"You should be proud," said Vena, "not ashamed. Not everyone can write."

"Judging from my book reviews it's not obvious that I can write, either."

Michele smiled at this. "And to think that Berengária was trying to blackmail us with our secrets. She had a whole list, you know. The police found it in her place. She was going to blackmail all of us."

"I heard about Ona. How she wanted her to pay ten thousand," said Marge.

"What was her secret?" asked Vena.

"I'm not sure," said Michele. "She hasn't told me."

"You were also on Berengária's list, Michele?" asked Marge.

"I was, yeah. My secret being that I can't cook. And of course that my brother-in-law killed my husband seven years ago. Though that wasn't much of a secret. More like a family skeleton we'd much rather leave in the closet, since it hasn't done anyone any good." The case had received a lot of press at the time, even though Michele's father-in-law had tried to pull a few strings to make sure the press coverage was buried. As it was, the scandal hadn't damaged the reputation of the Droba Group as much as Bill had feared, or scared away investors and customers. And eventually the story had gone away. Until Isobel had decided to write about it, and Berengária had tried to make money from it.

"It has to be Berengária who killed Isobel," said Marge. "Hasn't it?"

"I don't know," said Michele with a sigh. "The police aren't telling me anything. They're not even telling my father-in-law, even though he's already complained to the chief of police, to the mayor, and to every council member who will listen."

"But they arrested her," said Vena. "Which means they know something."

"They know she tried to blackmail Ona," said Michele. "And that's it."

Ona now entered the kitchen, looking bright-faced and happy. "Can I help?" she asked.

"Sure," said Marge, and assigned the former supermodel to tomato chopping duties. "You're looking happy today, Ona."

"That's because I am," said the model. "I did something I should have done a long time ago. I talked to my sister," she explained.

"Well, that's good, isn't it?" said Marge kindly.

"It was. There were some things I needed to tell her, and I finally did."

"And she took it well, I take it?"

"She did, yeah. She took it very well. Much better than I expected."

The woman was positively radiant, Michele decided, and

she was happy for her. At least someone in the house was having good things happen to them.

"And I hear they arrested your blackmailer," said Vena.

"Yeah. I was there," said Ona. "I hadn't expected it to be her, to be honest."

"I hadn't expected it to be Berengária either," said Michele. "She's worked for me for years. And now this." Which just goes to show you never really know a person.

"She must have seen an opportunity and taken it," said Vena.

"But how did she get a hold of Isobel's book?" asked Ona.

"Which is why it must be her who killed Isobel," Marge reiterated. "How else did she have Isobel's book containing all of our secrets? No, it must be her."

"But if it is her, then why are we still here?" asked Vena. "Why haven't they let us go?"

Michele shrugged. "Beats me. Nobody tells me anything."

"Is it true Perlita and Nathan are getting a divorce?" asked Ona, mercifully changing the subject. The death of Isobel was horrible, but incessantly talking about it wasn't going to bring her back, or allow them to process the terrible events.

"They've asked for separate rooms," said Michele as she studied a piece of veal and wondered how to go about turning it into something edible and perhaps even delicious. "Apparently they were both having an affair with the same woman."

"Oh, my God!" said Vena, clasping a hand to her face. "No way!"

"Yeah, some artist that Nathan was representing and Perlita was organizing a show for." Izzy Price had tried to further her career in a most creative way, but had only succeeded in destroying it. "They're talking through their lawyers."

"How can they talk through their lawyers when they're both staying under the same roof?" asked Marge.

"A lot of couples getting a divorce stay under the same roof," said Vena. "Not because they want to, but because they have to. With real estate prices going through the roof, and rent being as high as it is, not everyone has the luxury of moving out while they put the house up for sale."

"Maybe they'll reconcile," said Ona, who clearly had a romantic streak. "Maybe they'll realize they still love each other and they'll get back together."

"Maybe you should have been a marriage counselor," said Michele.

"I don't think so," said the model with a laugh. "I don't like lost causes!"

They all laughed at that, even though it wasn't all that funny. Michele thought about her own boyfriend, and how he'd proposed to her several times already. Only last week he brought up the subject again. But she'd married once, to Dean, and it had ended in tragedy. So she didn't want to do it again. A silly superstition, maybe, but she didn't want anything to happen to Chris. You just never knew.

"Okay, so what do I do with this?" she asked, holding up the veal.

"You bake it," said Ona. "Simple."

"Simple for you, maybe," said Michele, frowning darkly at the meat. "Maybe I could put it in the microwave?"

"Oh, my God!" said Ona. "Are you trying to poison us? Here, give it to me."

And as Michele watched the other ladies busily preparing dinner, she happily took a sip from her Chardonnay. "Anything else I can do?" she asked finally.

"You can bring us some of that," said Marge, indicating the glass.

"I can do that," she said. She might not be a great cook,

but she could pour a mean glass of white wine. And so soon the others had all been supplied with the same nectar of the gods that was in her own glass, and the lively conversation became even livelier. And when Perlita joined them, and started telling them the story of how she found out that her husband was having an affair, Marge asked if she could write her story. It was exactly the kind of thing Kitty Velvet would like.

CHAPTER 39

Berengária Morató had finally decided to talk. A perspicacious cop had found a USB stick wrapped in a plastic freezer bag concealed at the bottom of a flower pot. On the USB stick they'd found Isobel Droba's manuscript. Confronted with this evidence, the housekeeper cracked, and as Chase sat in front of her, the words rolled from her tongue with the same fervor as her erstwhile reticence.

Dooley had taken up position next to Odelia, and awaited further developments with as much eager anticipation as the detective himself.

"How did you know about the manuscript?" Chase wanted to know.

"I hear sisters talk," said the housekeeper in her trademark clipped tones. "Loud words—big fight. Michele want no book. Isobel say she want book. I'm curious. So I sneak into Isobel room when she out and copy book on stick. I hurry. I read book and see lots of secrets."

"And so you decided to make some money by blackmailing people."

"Not blackmail. I protect secrets. They pay me money for protection."

"One other thing. Did you write these notes yourself?" he asked, placing the three notes on the desk. "Your English in these notes is excellent."

The housekeeper beamed at what she considered a compliment. "I look up Google Translate. Good English, yes? I copy words from phone. Good English?"

"Good English, yes," Chase grunted. "Okay, so you took the book and you blackmailed Ona Konpacka. What else?"

"What else what? Nothing else. I tell you all what else, Mister Policeman!"

"Okay, so what happened on the night of Isobel's murder? Did you go into her room again? Did she catch you this time?"

"I don't go into room again. Only go into room one time." She thought for a moment. "I want go to room again. Book not finished. Book not ready. Only part of book on computer. I want rest of book, but Isobel not leave room so no chance."

"How do you know you only had part of the book?"

"Book say part one, part two, part three, part four. Ten parts. Only four parts on stick." She thunked her head. "Stupid me. I hurry, and now only four parts of book."

"So you missed a trick," said Chase, leaning back.

"I miss six parts of book," said Berengária, showing us she could count as well as blackmail people. She held up six fingers. "Six parts. Silly me."

"Okay, so here's what I think happened," said Chase. "You discovered that you'd only downloaded a part of the manuscript, so you wanted the rest also. You wanted the entire book, so you could blackmail a lot more people. You knew you had gold in your hands, only you wanted more gold—you wanted all the gold."

"I want all gold, yes," Berengária confirmed. "I like gold."

"So you went back into Isobel's room."

"I no go back. Isobel in room."

"She was, but you were hoping she wasn't."

The woman frowned. "She was in room."

"Yeah, but you didn't know that. You wanted the rest of that book. You *needed* the rest of that book. And so you took a chance. You took a risk. You went back to download the final parts, only this time Isobel caught you red-handed."

Berengária held up her hands. "Hands not red. Hands pink."

"Isobel caught you in the act," Chase went on doggedly.

"Act? What act?"

"And so you hit her. You hit her on the head and killed her. And as if that wasn't enough, you stomped on her with your stiletto heels until you were sure she was dead. What size shoes do you wear? Never mind, we've got your shoe collection." He checked his notes, and something didn't seem to compute for he frowned. "What did you do with the shoes, Berengária? Mh? And the club?"

"Club? What club?"

"The club you used to kill Isobel!" Chase suddenly thundered.

But Berengária wasn't impressed. She grinned at the cop. "You very angry man, Mr. Policeman. Maybe you kill Isobel. You kill Isobel with big club and big shoe!"

"Where are the shoes, Berengária! What did you do with them!"

"I wear shoe. What else?"

"And the club?"

"Tennis club?"

"No, not tennis club. The club you used to club Isobel to death."

"No club. No play tennis," said the woman with a curt shake of the head.

"He's not getting anywhere, is he, Max?" said Dooley.

"No, not exactly," I agreed. "And I have the impression that Berengária's shoe size doesn't match up with the footprints they found on Isobel's body either."

Dooley's eyes traveled to the housekeeper's feet. They were big feet, for a woman her size. Much bigger, presumably, than the stilettos the killer wore when he or she used them to kill their victim.

"I don't think she did it," said Dooley. "She's a blackmailer, not a killer."

"I think you're right, Dooley," I agreed. "I don't think she's our killer."

"Me no killer," Berengária confirmed when Chase tried to press her once again. "Me not angry person. Me like people. Like Isobel. She good person. Nice person."

Except she'd caused a lot of trouble for a lot of people, Isobel had. By insisting she reveal their secrets, even though they had told them to her in confidence. And in doing so, she had sealed her own fate.

"Okay, let's try a different tack," said Chase. "Where were you on the night Isobel was killed, Berengária?"

"Visit friend."

"Friend? What friend?"

"Friend reporter. Sell book."

"You were visiting a reporter so you could sell Isobel's book?"

"Big scoop," said Berengária. "Big money. Reporter very happy."

"What's the name of this reporter?" asked Chase. "And what time was this, exactly?"

"One o'clock," said Berengária. "I not want Michele see

me leave house. I sneak out middle of night to see reporter. Reporter happy to see me. Happy with book."

"Name of this reporter?"

"Dan Goory. Big reporter."

Chase jerked his head up, and looked at Odelia, or at least where he thought Odelia would be, behind the one-way mirror. Odelia, too, was surprised by this piece of news. Dan Goory was her boss, after all, and editor of the *Hampton Cove Gazette*.

"You tried to sell Isobel's book to Dan Goory? Dan Goory of the *Gazette*?" Chase wanted to know.

"Yes, Dan Goory Gazette. Good newspaper. Good for English. I study. Read Gazette and Odelia Poole. Good reporter. Good language. I learn and study." She nodded with satisfaction and crossed her arms in front of her chest. "You happy now, angry policeman? I tell you all. No more secrets."

To say that Chase was happy would be an overstatement. He did look surprised, though, or even flabbergasted. And as he left the interview room to confer with Odelia, I had the impression our next port of call was the *Gazette*.

CHAPTER 40

*D*an wasn't surprised to see us. In fact I had the impression the aged editor had been expecting us. His white beard waggled in a non-existent breeze as he placed his hands flat on his desk, regarding his visitors keenly.

"Yes, Berengária Morató came to see me. In the middle of the night, no less. But when she said it was the only time we could meet, and she had something very interesting to show me, I decided I would gladly give up my sleep for a chance to publish something truly remarkable: a sneak preview of Isobel Droba's biography. Only when she arrived, and showed me the manuscript, I realized she wasn't Isobel's official emissary, as she had somehow managed to convey, but had actually stolen the book from her employer without Isobel's permission."

"So what did you do?" asked Odelia anxiously.

"I told her no deal, of course," said Dan. "You know me, Odelia. I'm the old-fashioned kind of newspaperman. I don't go around paying for stolen property. My impression was that Berengária represented Isobel, and when I discovered that wasn't the case, I told her the deal was off the table, and threatened to tell Isobel. She wanted money, of course. Twenty-five thousand for the first part of the manuscript, and another twenty-five for the second part, which she said she could get any time. But I told her no dice. I deleted the manuscript from my computer, and sent the woman packing."

"And then you never had the chance to tell Isobel, because she was murdered that same night," said Chase, nodding.

"Yeah, unfortunately she was. Imagine my surprise when I heard the news in the morning."

"So why didn't you tell us?" asked Odelia. "You could have saved us a lot of trouble."

"But I did tell you," said Dan. "I wrote you an email."

"You did?" asked Odelia, taking out her phone. She did some deft finger work and moments later produced a soft gasp. "God, Dan, you're right. And I missed it."

"That's all right. You've been pretty busy, haven't you? Up to your ears in this murder business. How is the investigation going? Any news?"

"We're being led from one dead end to another," said Odelia.

"I know the feeling," said the editor sympathetically.

"Just to be sure: what time did you meet with Berengária?" asked Chase.

"Two nights ago at one o'clock. Here in my office. The meeting lasted one hour." He arched a bushy white eyebrow when Odelia and Chase both groaned in dismay. "Another dead end?" When they nodded dejectedly, he smiled. "My apologies."

While Odelia and Chase strengthened their tissues by having a bite to eat, Dooley and I wandered over to the General Store to have a chat with Kingman and strengthen our own tissues. Wilbur Vickery is one of those lucky people who have salespeople of every possible description representing all the known and even unknown brands knocking on his door and offering him their wares, and among those salespeople are plenty who have dog and cat food to share.

And since Wilbur is essentially a warmhearted and generous person, he doesn't mind sharing his wealth with Kingman and Kingman's friends. Also, who's the best judge of cat food? Not Wilbur, since humans aren't the primary target audience for Purina or Sheba, or even that Hill's Science stuff. So Kingman ends up the designated guinea pig, sampling every new brand on the market.

Lucky for us we only need one sniff to know if something is up to snuff. And the stuff Wilbur had on offer today passed the sniffing test with flying colors. After the morning we'd had—with several disappointments in the sleuthing department—we were famished, and ate our fill while Kingman watched on.

"I don't like it so much," he said. "But then I'm not big on fish."

"Don't pull my leg, Kingman," I said. "All cats like fish."

"Not me. I'm not a big fan of fish. Tastes fishy to me."

I couldn't tell if he was joking or not, so I refrained from comment. Besides, I was too busy scarfing down my fill of fish nuggets.

"So where is Brutus?" asked the big cat, glancing around nervously.

"Home," I said curtly.

"Not investigating with the rest of you?"

"Brutus is depressed," said Dooley.

"Why? What does he have to be depressed about?"

"The fact that you're having an affair with Harriet," I said.

"But I'm not!" Kingman cried. "How many times do I have to tell you! I'm not having an affair with Harriet. Not that I don't want to, obviously. But there's only one tom for Harriet and that's Brutus. No idea why, but there you have it. Harriet loves Brutus, and nothing I say or do will convince her otherwise."

"So you have tried?" I asked, giving him a censorious glance.

"Oh, absolutely. No harm in that, is there? But no such luck, fellas. The lady is devoted." He sighed as he placed his large head on his front paws. "So why Brutus should be depressed is beyond me, to be honest. He's managed to ensnare Hampton Cove's prettiest and most lovely queen, the lucky bastard."

He seemed sincere enough, so I decided to press him a little further. "So why have you and Harriet been meeting in secret?"

"I don't know what you're talking about, Max."

Now I knew he was lying. Something was going on, and if he wasn't having an affair with the fair lady, then what? But no matter how I pressed him on the matter, he wouldn't budge. Sworn to secrecy by Harriet, no doubt.

"We're your oldest friends, Kingman. You have to tell us."

"I don't have to tell you anything, Max," he said snippily. "And besides, what's it to you?"

"I'm concerned about Brutus's well-being," I said.

"Or you could admit that you're a nosy busybody."

"These nuggets are delicious, Kingman," said Dooley.

"I'm glad you like them. If you hadn't eaten them, Wilbur would have chucked them in the bin."

Upon hearing that, Dooley and I redoubled our efforts to

square away the rest of the provisions. I'm a cat who believes in not looking a gift horse in the mouth, you see, even if that mouth belongs to a fish nugget and not a horse.

"So about Brutus," I reiterated. "Did you—"

"Brad Pitt was in here yesterday," Kingman interrupted me, clearly having had enough of this Brutus and Harriet business.

"Brad Pitt!" Dooley cried. "What was he doing here?"

"Shopping for groceries, I presume. Even Brad Pitt has to eat, Dooley."

"I know, but I just figured he'd have people doing his shopping for him."

"Anyway," said Kingman, who didn't like being interrupted when he was telling one of his tall tales. "So Brad Pitt walks into the store, and he's wearing one of those long smelly raggedy overcoats. As if he picked it straight out of a dumpster. His hair is a mess, he's got this unruly beard, and generally he's looking like a bum. And he starts taking stuff from the racks, and stuffing it into his pockets. So Wilbur figures he actually is a bum, and he grabs him and throws him out!"

"He didn't recognize him?"

"No, sir, he did not. Wilbur is probably the only shop owner who's ever kicked a movie star out of his shop after mistaking him for a bum. So ten minutes later a big limo pulls to a stop in front of the store, and Brad Pitt steps out and walks up to Wilbur. He takes a hundred-dollar bill out of his wallet and stuffs it into Wilbur's shirt pocket. Wilbur, too stunned for speech, just goggles at the man. 'Just a small token of my appreciation,' says Pitt. Turns out he's playing the role of a hobo in his next movie, and he was doing research. Wilbur kicking him out gave him exactly the experience he needed to capture the essence of the part. He's even giving Wilbur a credit in the movie. As a consultant! And even after all of that, Wilbur still didn't recognize the guy! It was only when several customers came up to him and asked him about it, that the penny finally dropped. And now he's kicking himself. Says he should have asked for a selfie, which he could have used as free publicity for the shop. The silly ass."

As Kingman was telling the story, a penny dropped inside my own noggin. And now it was me goggling at Kingman, before thanking him profusely.

"You're welcome!" Kingman yelled after me as I hurried off. "Can you at least tell me what you're thanking me for! Max? Come back here, buddy! I'll tell you Harriet's big secret!"

CHAPTER 41

That night, Berengária was pottering about her apartment. The police had finally decided to let her go, since apparently they didn't have anything on her to keep her locked up. She would have to face charges on the blackmail business she was engaged in, but she was free pending a trial, the police figuring she wasn't a flight risk. And she wasn't. Where would she go? Her home was here, in Hampton Cove, even though she was now going to have a difficult time of it.

The apartment was a mess, but then the police had searched it thoroughly, looking high and low for evidence of the murder they had assumed she committed. Drawers had been pulled out, clothes strewn on the floor, her mattress had been cut open, her precious books were all over the place. It was terrible. Just such a big, big mess. It would take her days to clean it all up. Not to mention she would have to buy a new mattress. She wondered if the police would pay for the damage. She didn't think they would.

The story of her arrest had spread throughout the community like crazy, of course, and now that she was released, that particular piece of news had probably spread just as fast, the entire neighborhood now being aware of a criminal in their midst. She would have to move to a different part of town maybe, her landlord probably not happy that the apartment had been trashed, and that her tenant was a criminal.

She'd cleaned up a little, had prepared herself some dinner, and was now sitting in her living room, her feet tucked underneath her, watching television and sipping from a cup of hot cocoa and nibbling from a chocolate chip cookie. The light in the room was subdued, with only a small lamp next to the TV set providing illumination, and shadows played across the wall behind her, like a pantomime in black and white.

Her eyes slowly drooped closed. It had been a long and eventful day, with the arrest, and the subsequent interrogations, and finally being brought home in a police car, which was enough to telegraph to the neighborhood that she was in legal trouble—if the story of her arrest wasn't enough for that. The whole thing would be in the papers tomorrow, no doubt, splashed across the front page. And on social media. Maybe she would even have to delete her Facebook page.

And as she slowly nodded off, suddenly she thought she heard a squeaking sound. As if a window was being opened. She glanced in the direction of the kitchen, but saw nothing out of the ordinary. After a while, the hot cocoa did its soothing work, and she was drifting off again.

And that's when her head was suddenly yanked back violently, and her breath was caught in her throat! She wanted to yell out, but her larynx was being squeezed shut by whoever was behind her, strangling her! She tried to insert her fingers between the piece of string or cord and her neck, but it was no use.

Whoever the killer was, she was no match for the

powerful arms and hands. Almost as if her neck was caught in a vise!

But just as she was on the verge of passing out, the room was suddenly ablaze with light, and the sound of loud voices filled the air. The vicious and deadly pull on her throat dropped away, and she fell forward. And as she glanced behind her, gratefully sucking air into her lungs again, she saw that a masked figure was fighting a losing struggle with that big and burly cop who had arrested her.

More cops stormed into the room, clamoring loudly, and dragged the masked killer away from her and down to the ground, securing their hands behind their back. The mask was yanked off, and much to her surprise, she found herself staring into the face of... her employer!

She almost didn't recognize Michele, the woman's features contorted in anger as they were, but it was definitely her. But why? Why was she trying to kill her?

She would have asked the question, but her throat was still painful and sore. But then that other woman who'd apprehended her that afternoon joined her on the couch, and was speaking words of comfort, and said that a doctor was coming, and was muttering apologies and saying they should have gotten there sooner.

"But why?" she finally managed to croak hoarsely. "Why me?"

And that, it seemed, was quite a long story.

CHAPTER 42

We were all gathered in Marge and Tex's backyard, though the atmosphere was a little strained, I found. Harriet, for one, wasn't her usual ebullient self, and had hardly said a word all afternoon. And Gran was also acting a little strange, with her frequent outbursts inquiring about the whereabouts of little Grace! It spooked her daughter and granddaughter, who were wondering if the old lady's faculties were waning.

Brutus, meanwhile, was lying next to Dooley and me on the porch swing, looking like something the cat dragged in. What particular cat had done the dragging, I couldn't say, but he was even refusing food, which was a first.

And so with a morose Brutus on our left, and a subdued Harriet on our right, I was feeling the strain. And since nobody was asking me about the case, it was up to Odelia to tell the others about the stunning events that had taken place the night before. Charlene was there, of course, seated next to Uncle Alec, and providing a captive audience. And so was Scarlett Canyon, Gran's friend, who sat listening with gleaming eyes.

Tex and Marge had finally returned from their tennis week, and looked happy to be home again, and to be able to sleep in their own bed. The fact that they'd spent almost a week in the company of a murderer probably added to their relief.

"I don't get it," said Charlene. "Why did Michele kill her sister-in-law? Was it because Gavin had killed Michele's husband seven years ago? Out of revenge?"

"Well, that's exactly it," said Odelia. "It wasn't Dean who was killed by Gavin. It was the other way around. Dean killed Gavin, and then fled the country."

"I don't understand," said Marge. "Michele's husband killed Isobel's husband?"

"Exactly. And it was as Michele had said: the two brothers had been quarreling, mainly about the state of the company, which was on the verge of being snapped up in a hostile takeover, and was in bad financial shape. Gavin blamed Dean, and Dean blamed Gavin. But the truth of the matter is that the economy wasn't doing them any favors, and Bill stepping back had spooked some of the investors, and also some of their major clients, who'd canceled contracts."

"Always a tricky moment, when a company passes from one generation to the next," Uncle Alec said as he eyed the salad on his plate and didn't seem to like what he saw. Charlene had put him on a diet again, and he wasn't happy about it.

"Yeah, so the two brothers got into an argument that night, and things got violent, with some pushing and shoving. And that's when Gavin fell and hit the edge of Dean's desk, and died."

"Involuntary manslaughter," the Chief grumbled unhappily as he put a piece of lettuce into his mouth and grimaced.

"The problem was that Gavin's death would have meant

the end of the Droba Group for sure," Odelia continued her tale. "Dean would have gone to jail, and the group would have collapsed, and become a sitting duck for this corporate raider. So that's when Dean came up with the idea of the switch. He was the one with the very lavish life insurance contract to his name. So what if he was the one who was killed? That way Michele could collect the money, invest it in the group, and refinance the company so they could ward off that hostile takeover business."

"And so that's what they did," said Chase, munching on a nice chicken wing, unfazed by Uncle Alec's envious stares. "Dean was declared dead, and 'Gavin' fled the country, and since both Michele and Isobel had been present at the scene, they were the only ones, apart from Dean, who knew what had really happened. Michele identified the dead man as her husband Dean, and Isobel testified that her husband Gavin had accidentally killed his brother, and had escaped justice."

"Did Bill know?" asked Marge.

"Michele claims he didn't," said Odelia. "But I find that very unlikely. He must have had some involvement. It was his personal jet that was used to whisk Dean away, and Dean was able to set himself up as some kind of local real estate king in Belize, so he must have received a sizable sum of money—possibly from his dad."

"But Michele denies everything, and so does Bill," said Chase. "And we can't prove it, so..." He shrugged, and munched some more on that chicken wing, juice dripping down his chin, with the Chief looking on, transfixed and licking his lips.

"Okay, so why would Michele wait seven years to kill her sister-in-law? And why kill her at all?" asked Charlene.

Tex, who was manning the grill, waved his tongs. "The book, right? It must have been the book."

"It was the book," Odelia confirmed. "You see, Isobel had taken the death of her husband hard, and had started drinking. And it was only after becoming sober again that she realized she would never be able to get over Gavin's death unless the truth of what had actually happened was revealed. But when she told Michele what she planned to do, she was livid. Michael was gearing up to take over control of the group, and if it transpired that his dad was a murderer, not only would the insurance company kick up a fuss, and demand their money back, but Bill might be implicated, and Michele, and by extension Michael as well. And the last thing Michele wanted was for her son to get caught up in Dean's terrible mistake."

"And so to protect her son, Michele decided that Isobel had to die," said Chase, offering Uncle Alec a piece of chicken, fresh from the bone. The Chief's hand slowly stole out, but then he caught Charlene's look of disapproval, and he quickly retracted the hand, and shook his head. Instead he picked up a pickle.

"So it was Michele who used her stiletto on her sister-in-law?" asked Marge.

"Yes, she did. First she knocked Isobel over the head with a baseball bat that used to belong to Dean, and then she expended her rage on the woman by stomping on her several times, making sure she was dead. It was a frenzied attack, and shows just how mad she was with Isobel for wanting to destroy Michael's future by dragging up the past."

"Michele never liked Isobel," said Chase. "She told us as much. Said she was a weak and annoying whiny person, not fit to carry the proud Droba name. She was a disappointment to them all, and she was glad she was dead. Good riddance, were her exact words."

"Who wants meatballs!" Tex cried as he carried up a plate of the delicious treats.

"Ooh, I love a tasty meatball!" said Dooley.

"I thought you were a vegetarian?" Brutus grunted.

"I am a vegetarian, which is why I eat meatballs," said Dooley, showcasing his own unique brand of logic.

"So why did Michele attack Berengária?" asked Charlene.

"Because we had told her that we were releasing Berengária," said Chase. "And we also told her that Berengária was definitely in possession of Isobel's full manuscript, but we hadn't been able to find it so far. But we were hoping that Berengária would decide to cooperate, and share the manuscript with us."

"And of course Michele couldn't have that," said Odelia. "So she set out to kill Berengária, and make sure the manuscript was buried forever."

"You set her up," said Charlene.

"We did," Chase confirmed. "We told Michele and the others they were free to go, but we hadn't expected her to move so fast. Lucky for us—and Berengária—we got there just in time."

"So… the man who died in Belize was Dean Droba, and not Gavin?" asked Scarlett. She had been darting looks of concern at her friend Vesta, who hadn't said a word all afternoon, and just sat there with a sort of glazed look in her eyes.

"Yes, he was," Odelia confirmed.

"Did Michele know that her husband had died?"

"Yes, she did. They had kept in touch. And Michele regularly sent him pictures of the kids, especially Michael of whom Dean was particularly proud. But she said their marriage had run its course long before he left for Belize. He wasn't exactly known for his faithfulness, and she said he was having affairs all through their married life. So his death wasn't a great loss for her."

"It will come as a big shock to Michael and his sister," said Marge. "All these years they thought their dad was dead. And now all of a sudden it turns out that he was alive until three years ago."

"Same thing goes for Alison," said Charlene. "The dad she thought had fled to Belize in fact died seven years ago and was buried under his brother's headstone."

They were all quiet for a moment, as they thought about the fateful ruse Dean had orchestrated, with or without his father's assistance, and the wide-ranging ramifications, which reverberated until this day, and probably far beyond.

"Okay, so what's going on with you?" asked Odelia finally, addressing her grandmother. "You haven't said a word all afternoon, except to ask about Grace."

"Where is Grace!" Gran cried, coming out of her stupor.

"Grace is right there!" said Odelia, pointing to the little girl, who was playing on the porch.

"Oh," said Gran, and retreated into her shell once more.

"Are you all right, Vesta?" asked Chase with concern. "You don't look so hot."

Gran suddenly emerged from her lethargy. "Don't look so hot? You've got some nerve, sonny boy, talking to an old lady like that."

"No, it's just that I thought... that I figured... that I wondered..."

"What Chase is trying to say," said Uncle Alec, "is if you've finally lost your last marble."

Gran's frowned. "Now what a thing to say to your beloved mother."

"But it's true! You haven't been yourself, Ma. So what's wrong, huh?"

"Nothing is wrong," said Gran. "Just that I've been on a mission, that's all."

"What mission? What are you talking about?"

"A mission to try and make you see the light!"

"What light? Stop talking in riddles, will you!"

"Just look at that poor little girl, being dumped at that stupid daycare. You should be ashamed of yourselves, all of you! Children should be raised by their families, not by some strangers, surrounded by the whiny brats of other people."

"Those whiny brats are all friends of Grace now, Gran," said Odelia.

"That's right," said Chase. "She loves going to the daycare center."

"No, she doesn't. She has no other choice, cause you dump her there like an animal left at the pound. You even forget she exists, which is why I've been trying to scare you into remembering that you even have a daughter!"

"That's not fair, Ma," said Marge. "Odelia and Chase have been busy."

"They're always busy! And forgetting they've got a duty to their daughter!"

"A lot of working parents have kids, Ma. And they're doing just fine."

"Well, I wanted you both to stop and think for a minute. Odelia could give up that job of hers right now if she wanted to. Newspapers are a thing of the past anyway. People get their news from social media these days, not from a silly paper. And as far as Chase is concerned, Alec can find himself another detective. It's not safe for a dad to hobnob with criminals. Too dangerous! And the same goes for Odelia. So Odelia, quit your job, and Chase: get a desk job and work from home."

"Chase is not a desk jockey, Ma," Uncle Alec grunted irritably.

"Well, he should be. Much safer that way, and at least Grace will know who her dad is. Imagine her waking up one day when she's eighteen and wondering if her dad is the guy running the daycare center."

"I doubt she'll be at the daycare center when she's eighteen," said Odelia.

"You know what I mean. A child needs her parents. It's important."

"I know it's important, Gran," said Odelia. "And we're trying the best we can. But Grace also needs a roof over her head, and food on the table, and if I quit my job, and Chase takes a job he can do from home, how are we going to pay the bills? We're simply trying to balance work and family. It's not easy, but we're committed to doing the best we can. With your help, of course, and Mom and Dad."

"Money is not an object," said Gran airily. "It will come from somewhere."

"Unless Odelia wins the lottery, I doubt that very much," said Marge.

"Can I say something?" said Scarlett. "I've been watching Vesta this past week. She told me what she was planning, and I told her it was probably a bad idea, like a lot of her ideas. But Vesta being Vesta, she went ahead and did it anyway."

"Of course," said Gran.

"Look, I think you all love Grace very much. And you all want what's best for her. Each of you in your own way. And naturally there will be differences of opinion. But at the end of the day, I think it's important for you to understand, Vesta, that Chase and Odelia are great parents, trying hard to do the right thing."

"I'm not disputing that," said Gran with a shrug.

"So maybe work out some kind of schedule. Some days Vesta can take care of Grace, and some days I can. And some days she can go to daycare. It takes a village to raise a child, and I think that if you all sit down and talk about this, you'll see that it's not that hard to work something out."

"Isn't that what we're doing right now?" said Charlene.

"Yeah, I guess it is," said Gran. "Which is all I ever wanted."

And as the discussion turned lively, Uncle Alec took advantage of the mêlée to sneak a piece of chicken onto his plate and then into his mouth.

"Why is it so hard to raise a child, Max?" asked Dooley. "I mean, cats don't make such a big fuss, do they? They don't have daycare centers and concerned grandparents and aunts and uncles worrying over their every step."

"Cats are born pretty much fully formed, Dooley," I said. "With humans it takes years before they're ready to go out into the world. And even then it's touch and go sometimes." I shrugged. "Let's face it. Cats are the superior species." Okay, perhaps I was being a little harsh on our humans. But then I was disappointed that neither Odelia or Chase had credited me with providing the breakthrough that had solved their big murder inquiry. But then wasn't that often the case?

But before I could grump some more, Odelia approached, and placed some delicious pieces of glistening hot meatball in front of us. She then patted me on the head and said, "You did great, Max. Another case solved, and we couldn't have done it without you. Thanks, buddy."

"Yeah, thanks, Max!" Chase said, raising his glass to me.

And before I knew it, they were all raising their glasses to me, and thanking me for my most valuable contribution.

"Oh, you guys," I said, wiping away a tear.

Okay, so maybe humans are not so bad after all.

Later that night, to celebrate a job well done, the four of us went down to the park, this time not to catch a blackmailer, but to join cat choir. Brutus was walking behind us, and Harriet was walking in front of us, and the couple hadn't spoken now for days, it seemed. Frankly I won't conceal the fact that I was worried.

"How are we going to reconcile these two, Max?" asked Dooley.

"I have no idea," I said. I might be a good detective, but this case was too hard for me to solve.

We soon arrived at cat choir, and to my surprise, the members of dog choir were also present: Rufus, Fifi, and the others, all gathered in the playground.

Harriet quickly took up her position at the center of cat choir, a big smile on her face, and the moment Brutus finally showed up, dragging his paws, suddenly the entire choir erupted in a loud and cheerful, "Happy birthday, Brutus!"

And before the big cat knew what was happening, Harriet streaked forward, and placed a big smackeroo on his lips and said, "Happy birthday, boo bear!"

"But, but, but…" Brutus stuttered.

And he was still recovering from the surprise, when the two choirs burst into song, singing Céline Dion's *That's The Way It Is*, with Harriet taking care of the high notes, and the dogs doing those low ones that make all the difference.

When all was said and done, Brutus had been reduced to a blubbering mess of tears and gratitude, and was stammering, "Y-y-you guys!"

"That's why I was meeting with Kingman and Shanille," said Harriet as she gave her mate a loving nudge. "I was cooking up a surprise for your birthday!"

"Oh, baby girl!"

"Oh, little muppet!"

"Oh, kit kat!"

"Oh, chickadee!"

"God," I muttered. And as Harriet and Brutus went and

settled down so they could talk some more, I asked Shanille, "Why didn't you tell us, though? Brutus is our friend."

"I wanted to tell you," said Shanille. "But Harriet swore us to secrecy. She said you and Dooley are the best friends any cat could hope to have, but you have one big problem: you can't keep a secret."

"I can too keep a secret!" I cried, much offended.

"I also wanted to tell you, Max," said Kingman.

"And me," said Fifi.

"And me," said Rufus.

"Don't tell me. Harriet didn't want you to."

"Strict embargo," said Rufus.

"She made us promise," said Fifi.

"She made us swear on the heads of our children!" said Kingman.

"You don't have any children, Kingman," I said.

"Maybe I have, maybe I don't. It's a secret and I'll never tell, Max."

It made me wonder. Did Harriet have a point? Did I have a problem keeping things a secret? I didn't think so. Or did I?

But the occasion was too festive to fret, and soon I joined in the revels, as Brutus was being fêted by the entire Hampton Cove cat community, with selected representatives from the canine contingent. Fun was being had by all, and that was good enough for me. Maybe I wouldn't have been able to keep my mouth shut. Maybe watching Brutus suffer would have been too much for me to bear, and I would have put him out of his misery by revealing the big secret. Who knows?

"I think we can keep a secret, Max," said Dooley at the end of the night, when we were making our way back to the old homestead. "But sometimes we choose not to, because not keeping it is better than keeping it. We're smart that way."

"You think so?"

"Oh, sure. You're very smart, Max. And sometimes secrets aren't worth keeping, if a person is suffering because of it. Like with Brutus this week."

I smiled at my friend. He was right. Sometimes revealing a secret is the right thing to do. And sometimes it isn't. And knowing the difference is the big trick.

"So maybe you can finally tell us *your* secret, Brutus," I said.

"Yes, cuddle bug," said Harriet. "What's your big secret?"

Brutus smiled. "It's not much of a secret, really, except..."

"Except? Come on, babes, don't keep us in suspense."

"Okay, here goes." He took a deep breath. "When I squint my eyes, my butt itches."

We all stared at him. "*That's* your big secret?"

Brutus shrugged. "I told you it wasn't much."

"Can you demonstrate, Brutus?" asked Dooley. "Just to give us an idea?"

And so Brutus gave his best Clint Eastwood impersonation, then scratched his butt to prove his point.

Dooley was laughing his own butt off. "Best. Secret. Ever!" he said.

We'd arrived home, and jumped up on the low wall that borders the front yard. Harriet and Brutus gazing up at the full moon and mooning over each other. And Dooley wondering if the moon was made of cheese, and if it was, how it tasted. And me? I was happy to be in the company of such great friends. Cause if Harriet thought I couldn't be trusted with a secret, out of fear I'd tell Brutus, what she was really saying was that I loved my friends so much I couldn't see them suffer.

And when you come right down to it, that's quite a compliment, isn't it?

THE END

Thanks for reading! If you want to know when a new Nic Saint book comes out, sign up for Nic's mailing list: nicsaint.com/news

EXCERPT FROM PURRFECT BOUQUET (MAX 56)

Chapter One

Cat choir is one of those laid-back affairs I very much look forward to each and every day. In fact if it weren't for cat choir, I don't know if my life would be half as enjoyable as it is now. Now don't be fooled by the addition of the word 'choir' in cat choir. I know it looks like a choir when a bunch of cats get together to mewl and meow and generally make a huge caterwauling nuisance of themselves, but in actual fact the singing is a mere excuse for us to socialize and shoot the breeze.

And so it was that the sun had finally set on a glorious day, and that our humans were getting ready to go to bed. Teeth were being brushed, the closing credits on movies and TV shows were rolling, curtains were being pulled, and amid all this hubbub and activity, cats were using the opportunity to gobble up those final pieces of kibble, emptying those bowls before leaving the house and making their trek to the local park. Some of them made a detour, to chase some

EXCERPT FROM PURRFECT BOUQUET (MAX 56)

critter or sharpen those claws on some nearby tree, but in due course Hampton Cove's cat population made its way en masse to the place to be: cat choir.

For as long as I remember, Shanille has led cat choir and has done an excellent job at it, too. Shanille is Father Reilly's cat, you see, and since St. John's Church boasts a long choral tradition, she must have gotten the idea from the great man himself. And very creative she is, too. Always has some new songs she wants us to try out, some new ideas she's come up with. In fact it isn't too much to say that Shanille lives and breathes cat choir. In other words: she is cat choir personified.

Which is why it came as something of a shock to us when we arrived at the park and discovered that Shanille wasn't amongst those present at all!

We rehearse in the park's playground, you see. During the daytime the place is filled with the sounds of frolicking kids having fun, but at night it's our turn, much to the neighbors' chagrin, I might add. Oddly enough the same category of people who hate kids also seem to hate cats, but still prefer living in houses overlooking playgrounds and places where kids and cats like to gather. I guess they must be closet masochists, but don't quote me on that since I'm not a licensed shrink.

As I looked around now, I saw that the jungle gym was there, and so was the seesaw, the swing and the merry-go-round, but of our illustrious and indefatigable conductor there was not a single trace—Shanille was late!

"Where is Shanille, Max?" asked Dooley, who'd also become aware of the marked absence of one usually so undeniably and emphatically present.

"I have no idea," I admitted.

"Maybe she's been delayed," Brutus suggested.

EXCERPT FROM PURRFECT BOUQUET (MAX 56)

"Or maybe she's sick," Harriet said, a touch of hope in her voice.

Harriet and Shanille's relationship may best be described as fraught with a certain measure of rivalry. They both consider themselves Hampton Cove's First Feline Females or FFF's, and as we all know you can't have two FFF's, the same way you only have one BFF. Their former enmity has morphed into a tenuous truce, especially since they both have important roles to play that they've claimed for their own: Shanille as cat choir's fearless leader and grande dame and Harriet as its lead soprano, also known as its prima donna.

I guess you could argue that you can't have two divas in the same ensemble, but so far Shanille and Harriet have managed to make it work. In a sense.

"I bet she'll show up soon," I said, trying to take the optimistic view.

"And I'll bet she's home being sick as a dog," said Harriet with relish.

"Why do they always say 'sick as a dog,' Max?" asked Dooley. "Why not sick as a cat, or sick as a rabbit? Is it because dogs are more often sick than we are?"

"I'm not sure," I said. The matter wasn't my top priority at that moment. Locating Shanille was. For a choir without a conductor isn't much of a choir at all.

"If she doesn't show up soon, we won't have a choir tonight!" said Brutus.

"She'll show up," I said. "She has to." In all the time I'd known her, Shanille had never missed a rehearsal even once.

"Do you think we can be sick as dogs?" asked Dooley, who liked to march to the beat of his own drum. "Cats aren't dogs. So we can't be sick like dogs, can we?"

"No, I guess we can't," I said.

EXCERPT FROM PURRFECT BOUQUET (MAX 56)

"We can be 'sick as a cat,'" he continued. "But not 'sick as a dog' or 'sick as a rabbit,' or even 'sick as a mouse.' It just stands to reason, doesn't it?"

"It does," I said, though I was starting to find this conversation a little trying.

"Oh, there she is," said Brutus, as a feline female hove into view.

"That's not Shanille," said Harriet. "That's Samantha."

"Oh, right."

And so the long wait began. I'm not sure if you know this, but not all cats possess the virtue of patience. Harriet, for one, most definitely does not, and neither does Brutus. Dooley, because he often inhabits an alternate universe, is better equipped to deal with these matters. As for myself, I find that it helps if you think of something else entirely. And so I started to imagine what I would find in my food bowl when we got home that night. Odelia likes to change things up, you see. She knows that always eating the same thing gets tedious after a while.

"Look, it's Kingman," said Brutus, causing me to emerge from that perennial discussion about whether I like chicken best or turkey.

Kingman now came waddling up to us, looking distinctly distraught.

"The worst thing happened!" he cried even before he reached us.

"What's wrong?" asked Dooley immediately. "Has the world ended?!"

"No, the world hasn't ended," said Kingman, breathing stertorously as he plunked himself down. "But it wouldn't surprise me if it does. Shanille is gone!"

"Gone? What do you mean, gone?" I asked.

"I dropped by the church earlier, so we could walk here together, as we often do, and she wasn't there!"

EXCERPT FROM PURRFECT BOUQUET (MAX 56)

I relaxed. This wasn't as bad as I thought. "That doesn't mean she's gone, Kingman. That means she's gone out somewhere."

"But Shanille never goes out! Where would she even go?!"

He was right, of course. Cats rarely go places. We're your essential homebodies, never happier than adhering to our fixed routines and enjoying the creature comforts of our own wonderful little homes.

"Maybe Father Reilly decided to take a vacation?" I ventured.

The large cat gave me a look of exasperation. "Father Reilly never goes on vacation! His parishioners need him! Just like cat choir needs Shanille!"

"Maybe they've been abducted by aliens," Dooley suggested. "Or maybe Father Reilly has gone to Rome. Don't priests go to Rome to be with the Pope?"

"They do," Kingman confirmed, "but at least she could have told me!"

"Could be that Shanille had an accident," said Harriet with a light shrug.

"I say we organize a search party," said Brutus. "Save Shanille!"

"I'm sure she'll be here any moment," I said, trying to inject some reason into the conversation, which was getting a little out of hand, I felt.

More cats had turned up, and the sound of nervous conversation filled the air. The distinct lack of conductor hadn't escaped anyone's attention, and cats being cats, all possible explanations were being entertained. Shanille had joined a cult and moved to India. Or Shanille had been abducted and was being held for ransom by a gang of catnappers. Though the most original theory was that she had been snapped up by Hollywood, and had moved to LA to star in a movie about her life.

EXCERPT FROM PURRFECT BOUQUET (MAX 56)

"As if," Harriet scoffed when this possibility was suggested to her. "Shanille's life isn't interesting enough to be turned into a movie." She cleared her throat and raised her voice. "Listen up, you guys! Unfortunately Shanille won't be joining us tonight. So as her second-in-command I'm going to take over. If you could please all take your positions, we'll start with some warm-up exercises for the voice!"

These warm-up exercises apparently consisted of using the full range of our vocal cords and projecting as loudly as possible and as far as possible. The upshot was that within five minutes windows on all sides of the park were being opened, angry heads were being thrust out, and voices were raised in anger, with a few of those hanging from their windows even throwing the odd shoe in our direction.

Personally I wouldn't have minded being pelted in the lower back with a nice sneaker—an Air Jordan, for instance, or an Allen Edmonds. I could even go for a soft Yeezy. But instead I got an old army boot for my trouble. It was big and bulky—not to mention smelly—and not a nice way to start the evening!

Around me, more footwear started raining down, causing cat choir to cut its session short for once. And so Harriet's vocal warm-up exercises, which had sounded like such a good idea, turned out not to be such a good idea after all. And when a police siren sounded in the distance, drawing closer, we decided to skedaddle.

"I hope Shanille is all right," said Dooley as we made a run for it.

"I'm sure she is," I said, as I dodged a pair of Chuck Taylors.

This unexpected hailstorm of shoes didn't bode well for the future, though.

"This is an outrage," Harriet gasped as she barely escaped

EXCERPT FROM PURRFECT BOUQUET (MAX 56)

an incoming Mary Jane. "We should file a complaint against these people! For assault and battery!"

"I'm not sure throwing a shoe at a cat is in the penal code," I said.

"Well, it should be! If they can't guarantee our safety, at the very least they should give us our own rehearsal space. A nice big conference hall, for instance."

Somehow I doubted whether the powers that be could be enticed to give the cats of Hampton Cove access to a conference hall. Then again, I wouldn't want to spend all my nights indoors. Part of why I like cat choir so much is that it takes place in the great outdoors.

"Maybe we should move to the woods," Brutus suggested as he ducked an Ugg. "Plenty of space out there, and no annoying neighbors to give us any grief."

"I don't like the woods," Dooley intimated with a shiver. "They're dark and creepy and full of animals!"

"You're an animal, Dooley," Brutus reminded him. "We're all animals."

"Yeah, but the animals that live in the woods are wild animals!"

He had a point, of course. After millennia of sharing humans' homes I guess we have become domesticated to some extent. Being released into the wild would come as a big shock to most of the members of cat choir. Having to fend for ourselves, and forage for food and such. "Dooley is right," I said therefore. "The woods are no place for a couple of nice, civilized cats like us. The woods are dangerous, and full of wild creatures who wouldn't take kindly to our presence."

You'll be gratified to know that we finally made it out of the park alive, though it was a narrow escape. And as we wended our way home, Dooley reminded us of more pressing matters than escaping these shoe-throwing anti-cat zealots.

"We have to find Shanille," he said. "She could be in big trouble."

Chapter Two

Marge Poole was surprised to find that she was the first one out of bed that morning. When she arrived in the kitchen and didn't find her mom sipping from a cup of coffee, she glanced through the window, but instead of the usual sight of Vesta pottering about in the backyard, busy with her trowel and her flowerbeds, the old lady wasn't anywhere to be seen. Usually an early riser, Marge's mom wasn't in the living room either, nor had she taken the car and gone for a drive.

Figuring she'd probably gone for a stroll, Marge went about her business of getting ready for her day. And she'd already prepared breakfast and put a wash on when she wandered into the bedroom and saw that her hubby was still sound asleep, which was not his habit.

"Rise and shine, sleepyhead," she called out therefore.

Tex mumbled something, then turned and went straight back to sleep.

Walking into her mother's bedroom to put the laundry away, she discovered to her surprise that her mother was still in bed! Now that was odd—very odd!

"Ma, time to get up," she said, as she opened the curtains with a vigorous movement and stood staring out through the window for a moment, as one does.

Behind her, nothing stirred, and when she glanced over, she saw that her mother hadn't moved an inch. She was sleeping on her back, her mouth half open.

A sudden fear gripped Marge, and she crossed the

EXCERPT FROM PURRFECT BOUQUET (MAX 56)

distance to the bed in two seconds, then stared down hard at the gray-haired old lady. But her chest was still rhythmically rising and falling, and soft snores emanated from her lips, so Marge relaxed, stilling her wildly beating heart and telling herself not to be silly. Her mother might not be as young as she liked to think, but she wasn't that old either!

It was ten minutes later when she was taking an empty bottle into the garage and opening the appropriate receptacle so she could deposit it amongst its discarded colleagues when she saw no less than three wine bottles in the bin.

She blinked. Now where had those come from? She wasn't a big drinker, and as far as she knew, neither was Tex. Though it was true that lately he'd started drinking more. An aperitif before dinner, some wine with his meal, and sometimes when they were watching TV he'd have another. But that still didn't explain these empty bottles, so the only person who could have put them there was her mother. Which might go a long way to explaining why she was still in bed instead of getting up at the crack of dawn as she usually did.

Three bottles—but she couldn't possibly have drunk all three of them last night, could she?

Marge thought hard. When was the last time she had looked into this bin? Must have been a couple of days ago—a week at the most. Still, three bottles in perhaps just as many days? That was one bottle of wine per evening!

Time to have a little talk with her mother about her drinking habits!

꿏

As Dooley and I accompanied our human to work—work for Odelia, that is, nap time for us—my mind was still busy trying to come up with a reason for Shanille's absence last night.

EXCERPT FROM PURRFECT BOUQUET (MAX 56)

There could be a perfectly simple explanation, of course. In fact this idea of Father Reilly having gone on holiday and deciding to take his cat along was the most probable one. You see, Father Reilly, against the strictures of his church, had consorted with his housekeeper Marigold—if consort is the word I want—and from this illicit union in due course offspring had sprung.

The good priest, now having a little flock of his own to care for, had decided not so long ago to be a man of the cloth no more, and to leave his bigger flock of parishioners to some as yet unknown successor. All this so he could make an honest woman out of Marigold. And what do humans do when they have a wife and kids? They go on holiday. And if they're halfway decent humans beings, like Father Reilly most certainly is, they take their pets along with them.

So that's what must have happened. And in spite of Kingman's protestations that Shanille would have told him if such was the case, perhaps Shanille hadn't known herself that these plans were being made. Unlike Odelia some pet parents don't bother consulting their pets when they make their holiday plans, you see. One moment you're happily dozing in your favorite spot, and the next you're being shoved into a pet carrier and taken along on some long-haul holiday!

But even as we settled down in our corner of the office, ready to while away the morning by taking a nice long nap, I wondered if we shouldn't be out there looking for our friend. This holiday thing was all well and good, but cats being cats, someone would have seen them leave on this much-coveted outing. So shouldn't we at least ask around? Put our minds at ease? But then I decided that Shanille wouldn't want that. She wouldn't want her friends getting all worked up and roaming the streets trying to find her.

"I think Shanille must have found herself a different choir," said Dooley, whose mind had been working along

EXCERPT FROM PURRFECT BOUQUET (MAX 56)

more or less the same lines as mine, but had clearly arrived at a different conclusion. "Remember how she told us two nights ago that we didn't have what it took? That we were a bunch of amateurs and why was she wasting her great talent on the likes of us?"

I frowned at my friend. "I'd totally forgotten about that," I admitted.

"She even said that by rights she should have been snapped up by now by some enterprising impresario to conduct an internationally-renowned choir."

"It's true," I said. "She even said she might look for one herself." Immediately my mood lightened to a not inconsiderable degree. "Yes, that must be it. She must have gone to look for some prestigious choir to conduct. Some famous outfit."

Something along the lines of the Cornell University Choir. Or the Tabernacle Choir at Temple Square. These were the kinds of choirs Shanille often referred to, claiming they were the absolute tippity top, and something for us to aspire to, before throwing up her paws in despair when we actually started singing.

"Oh, well," said Dooley. "Harriet will have to fill in for now, won't she?"

My mood dropped again, and I rubbed the painful spot in my rear where that big boot had connected. "If Harriet becomes the new conductor of cat choir we're going to have to get Odelia to buy us a suit of armor," I grumbled. "To protect us from the shoes these darn neighbors will be throwing at us."

"We could always skip the vocal warm-up," Dooley suggested.

And I'm sure a lot more could have been said on the topic, but at that moment a couple walked into the office, and

EXCERPT FROM PURRFECT BOUQUET (MAX 56)

asked if they could have a word with our human. So we pricked up our ears, and switched to listening mode.

"Sure," said Odelia pleasantly, and offered the couple a seat. "What can I do for you?"

They were both fairly young. Early to mid-twenties at the most. And they were a handsome couple, the woman fair-haired and blue-eyed, and the man dark-haired and brown-eyed. They looked athletic and were dressed in casual clothes: jeans and sweaters.

"We have a problem," the man said. "And we've been told that you might be able to help us."

He spoke with a faint accent which, if I wasn't mistaken, could have been French.

"Maybe we should introduce ourselves first," said the woman. "My name is Stephanie Felfan—though everyone calls me Steph. And this is my husband Jeff Felfan."

"Odelia Kingsley," said Odelia. "But I'm guessing you already knew that."

"The thing is," said Steph, "that I'm in something of a pickle. You see, I'm a fashion designer, or at least that's what I want to be. It's what I studied. And recently a job became available at one of the country's hottest new fashion labels, WelBeQ, which is located in LA. So I sent in my resume and as you can imagine I was over the moon when they offered me the position. Assistant to the head designer at WelBeQ. So a week passes, and we're already making all the necessary arrangements, when suddenly I get an email that they've changed their mind, and that they're going in a different direction. I ask them what happened, but total radio silence. They won't respond to my emails, when I try to call them I can't get anyone on the phone. Complete blackout. So I'm shocked, right? Of course I am."

"What is a welbeck, Max?" asked Dooley, interrupting Steph's story.

"A famous fashion brand," I said.

"I've never heard of it."

"Me neither," I said.

At the sound of our voices, Steph smiled and glanced in our direction. "Oh, will you look at those two cuties! Are they yours?"

"They are," said Odelia. "The big one is Max, and the smaller one is Dooley."

"They're absolutely adorable," said Steph. "Aren't they adorable, Jeff?"

"Very adorable," said Jeff, and pronounced adorable the way the French do.

"My husband is French," Steph explained. "We met in Paris, when I studied at the fashion academy there."

"Oh, so you're also a fashion designer?" asked Odelia.

"Oh, no," said Steph with a laugh.

"I'm a banker," said Jeff. "Not one ounce of designer blood."

"We like to joke that he'll bankroll me so I can start my own label."

"But I'm not a very good banker, I'm afraid," said Jeff. "I'm a poor banker. I don't have the money to bankroll Steph's career. But maybe one day."

"Jeff works for the Capital First Bank in Manhattan," Steph explained.

"As a lowly employee," said Jeff. "Not the bank's manager, unfortunately."

As it transpired, the couple had met in Paris, but had soon moved to New York, where Jeff found a well-paying job with the main branch of Capital First Bank. But even though they lived in the fashion capital of the country, Steph's dream was to move back to France and work for one of the big labels in Paris.

EXCERPT FROM PURRFECT BOUQUET (MAX 56)

"But you're not originally from Paris, are you?" asked Odelia.

"Oh, no. My parents live in Hampton Cove," said Steph. "Ian and Raimunda Stewart? They run the Stewart Winery, one of the biggest on Long Island."

"Oh, right!" said Odelia. "Of course. I did a piece on your family's winery once."

"I know," said Steph with a smile. "My mom framed it and put it on the wall of her office. She does the winery's PR, while my dad runs the company, along with my brother Kevin."

"But you're not bitten by the wine bug?"

"Absolutely not. I don't know why, but I always wanted to be a designer. And lucky for me Mom and Dad have supported me from the start to follow my own heart and carve my own path, and not feel obligated to follow in their footsteps."

"Okay, and so now you want to move to LA and start to work for WelBeQ and for some reason they first hired you, then changed their mind," said Odelia.

"That's right. And the worst part was that they wouldn't tell me why. So I finally decided to drop it, figuring maybe it just wasn't for me. And then yesterday, out of the blue, I get a call from someone who works in the HR department at WelBeQ. It wasn't an official call, and she wouldn't give me her name, but she read my emails, and said she was under strict instructions from the legal department not to respond. But she must have felt sorry for me, which is why she called." She took a deep breath. "Turns out someone launched a smear campaign against me."

"Someone did what?" asked Odelia, her astonishment obvious.

"A smear campaign. In the final round, there were only two candidates left for the job: me and a guy called Edmundo

Crowley. And so when they selected me, someone sent them a bunch of pictures of me, passed out drunk on the couch, Zoe on the floor next to me."

"Zoe?"

"Our baby girl," said Steph. "She'll be nine months next week." A brief smile flitted across her face. "For the record, I never, ever passed out drunk—ever. These pictures are obviously doctored. They were sent from an anonymous email account, and the story they were trying to convey was that I'm an unfit mother, an alcoholic, that I was a troublemaker, and probably a drug addict."

"Did she send you the email?"

"She did. It's disgusting—and completely fake, of course. But from their point of view I can understand why they decided to go with the other candidate."

"Who sent the email? Any idea?"

"I have a pretty good idea who sent it," said Steph, her expression hardening.

"Crowley," said Jeff. "He is the candidate Steph was competing against."

"He's the one who got the job when they ditched me," Steph clarified. "And I'm pretty sure he's the one who launched this campaign against me to damage my reputation. I mean, who else can it be?"

"Did the person who called you tell you this?" asked Odelia.

"I asked her, and she said she couldn't be one hundred percent sure, but she thought it must be Crowley. At least that's the consensus among her colleagues."

"There must be something you can do. Did you sign a contract?"

"Verbal agreement only. I was going to sign the contract on my first day."

"I see," said Odelia thoughtfully. "So what—"

"I want you to look into this email business. Find out who's behind it. And if it is Crowley I want to expose him, and file a complaint against him. And then I will go to WelBeQ and tell them what's going on."

"You still want to work for them?"

"Of course! This is my dream job. WelBeQ may not be one of the major fashion houses, but they have a great reputation as an innovative brand. They just might be the next Fenty. You know, Rihanna's brand? And if I can get in from the start, it's going to do wonders for my career. So yeah, I still want to work for them. And I want to prove that they picked the wrong candidate."

"It's not right that this Crowley got in by slandering Steph's reputation," said Jeff. "And if WelBeQ thinks she's an unreliable person, they might spread the word and talk to other companies, and very soon she will become unhirable."

"Which is why I want you to find out if it's really Edmundo Crowley who's behind this," said Steph. "To prove it somehow, so I can do something about it."

Chapter Three

"It's a nasty business, Max," said Dooley. "Slandering the reputation of a nice girl like Steph. Who would do such a thing? It's not okay."

I smiled. "You're absolutely right, Dooley. It's not okay."

"And all this just to get a job. There should be a law against that kind of thing."

"I'm sure there is. But first we need to figure out who's behind this campaign."

A day had passed since Steph and Jeff had paid us a visit in the office, and now we were in the car with Odelia, cruising along the Long Island Expressway and making great progress. Odelia's old pickup was being overtaken by bigger,

EXCERPT FROM PURRFECT BOUQUET (MAX 56)

faster, newer cars, but she didn't mind. As long as it got us from point A—Hampton Cove—to point B—the residence of Edmundo Crowley—that was all that mattered.

The moment Steph and Jeff Felfan had left the office, Odelia had consulted with her editor Dan Goory. The white-bearded newspaperman had given his wholehearted approval to do what lay in our power to help the Felfans. They both sniffed a great story, and if it tied in with the Stewart Winery, that was even better. They might be able to launch a series of articles about the incident.

Odelia had phoned Mr. Crowley, and the man had agreed to do an interview. In fact it wasn't too much to say he was flattered when a reporter called him and complimented him on his achievements as a budding designer. A little flattery never hurts when talking to ambitious people like Steph's alleged nemesis.

"Are you sure you shouldn't have asked Chase to come along?" asked Dooley. "Just in case this Mr. Crowley proves to be a dangerous individual, I mean?"

"I doubt that he's dangerous," said Odelia. "He's a fashion designer, not an ax murderer."

"One doesn't exclude the other," Dooley insisted. "But just so you know: Max and I have your back, Odelia. The moment the man turns homicidal, we'll pounce."

"Good to know," said Odelia with a smile.

I have to say I admired her courage. It's not always easy to go and talk to complete strangers. You never know what you'll find. Like Dooley said, maybe reporters should travel in pairs, just like police officers, just in case.

Edmundo Crowley lived in Brooklyn, though if Steph was to be believed, not for very much longer. In fact we probably caught him just in time, as he was moving to LA soon, to start work for WelBeQ. A quick perusal of the man's apartment, once we got there, bore out my theory: suitcases

EXCERPT FROM PURRFECT BOUQUET (MAX 56)

were on his bedroom floor, his cupboards looked as if they'd been ransacked, clothes strewn about indiscriminately, and generally the place looked as if a minor tornado had recently landed there and done some serious damage.

"Moving, Mr. Crowley?" asked Odelia, showing what a keen reporter's eye she had. She was sitting in front of the young man, tablet in hand, ready to write down the pearls of wisdom that were about to fall from the designer's lips. Contrary to the state of his lodgings, the designer himself looked more like an accountant than a hot young artiste. Perhaps for this special occasion, he was dressed in an off-white shirt and tie and perfectly pressed and creased black pants, and even his shoes looked polished. He wore designer glasses and his hair was neatly coiffed.

"Yes, I'm sorry about the mess," he said, taking a seat. "I'm starting a new job soon, so I've been packing."

"A new job. Isn't that exciting?"

"Yeah, I was accepted at WelBeQ," said Edmundo with not a little bit of pride. "They're one of the hottest new brands on the market, but I'm sure you know all about that, being a fashion reporter and all."

Odelia smiled a sweet smile. "About that, I was contacted recently by Stephanie Felfan. I don't know if you've heard of her?"

The transformation was remarkable. The kind demeanor was instantly replaced by a cagey expression. "Stephanie Felfan?" he asked with a touch of suspicion.

"Yes, she was also in the running for the job at WelBeQ, same as you. She was even accepted and was offered the position. But then suddenly she got a message that there had been a mistake, and that she wasn't moving to LA after all."

"I see," said the young man, as he pushed his glasses up his nose. "I'm afraid I've never heard of this person. Stephanie Felfan, did you say?"

EXCERPT FROM PURRFECT BOUQUET (MAX 56)

"That's right. So Stephanie did a little digging, and turns out that you took the job that was initially promised to her. And what's more, the reason WelBeQ decided to go in a different direction is because some very damaging information about Stephanie found its way into their mailbox."

The man frowned in confusion. "Is that so?"

"It is. And what's more, she seems to think that one of the other candidates may have launched a smear campaign against her, trying to remove her from the equation. And so obviously this has her wondering who this person might be."

"Of course," said Edmundo, nodding. "If something like that happened to me, I'd also want to know who was behind it." He shrugged. "It's all news to me, I'm afraid, Mrs. Kingsley. No one at WelBeQ told me anything about the other candidates. I never even met the people at WelBeQ face to face, since everything was done over Zoom. So I'm afraid I can't help you." The frown returned. "So... if I understand you correctly, you're here on behalf of this... Stephanie Felfan?"

"Yes, I am," said Odelia. "Steph had her hopes set on this job, you see, and when it fell through, she was devastated."

"Oh, but I understand," said Edmundo, nodding. "It's a great opportunity."

"So... you're saying you don't know anything about this smear campaign?"

"That's correct," Edmundo confirmed. "I don't know anything about it. They kept us totally in the dark about the other candidates or even if there were other candidates. I assumed there were, of course, since the opportunity was so great, but as I said, I never met any of them and didn't even know their names."

"I understand," said Odelia thoughtfully.

I had the impression that the designer was a little disappointed that the reporter hadn't come to ask him about his stellar career as a promising young talent. But if he was, he was exceedingly decent about it. "It must have come as a great shock to your friend that she wasn't hired by WelBeQ," he said kindly. "And if I were in her shoes, I'd probably want to know what happened, too."

"It was her dream job," said Odelia simply.

"As it is for me," said Edmundo.

ABOUT NIC

Nic has a background in political science and before being struck by the writing bug worked odd jobs around the world (including but not limited to massage therapist in Mexico, gardener in Italy, restaurant manager in India, and Berlitz teacher in Belgium).

When he's not writing he enjoys curling up with a good (comic) book, watching British crime dramas, French comedies or Nancy Meyers movies, sampling pastry (apple cake!), pasta and chocolate (preferably the dark variety), twisting himself into a pretzel doing morning yoga, going for a run, and spoiling his big red tomcat Tommy.

He lives with his wife (and aforementioned cat) in a small village smack dab in the middle of absolutely nowhere and is probably writing his next 'Mysteries of Max' book right now.

www.nicsaint.com

ALSO BY NIC SAINT

The Mysteries of Max
Purrfect Murder
Purrfectly Deadly
Purrfect Revenge
Purrfect Heat
Purrfect Crime
Purrfect Rivalry
Purrfect Peril
Purrfect Secret
Purrfect Alibi
Purrfect Obsession
Purrfect Betrayal
Purrfectly Clueless
Purrfectly Royal
Purrfect Cut
Purrfect Trap
Purrfectly Hidden
Purrfect Kill
Purrfect Boy Toy
Purrfectly Dogged
Purrfectly Dead
Purrfect Saint
Purrfect Advice
Purrfect Passion

A Purrfect Gnomeful
Purrfect Cover
Purrfect Patsy
Purrfect Son
Purrfect Fool
Purrfect Fitness
Purrfect Setup
Purrfect Sidekick
Purrfect Deceit
Purrfect Ruse
Purrfect Swing
Purrfect Cruise
Purrfect Harmony
Purrfect Sparkle
Purrfect Cure
Purrfect Cheat
Purrfect Catch
Purrfect Design
Purrfect Life
Purrfect Thief
Purrfect Crust
Purrfect Bachelor
Purrfect Double
Purrfect Date
Purrfect Hit
Purrfect Baby
Purrfect Mess
Purrfect Paris

Purrfect Model

Purrfect Slug

Purrfect Match

Purrfect Game

Purrfect Bouquet

The Mysteries of Max Box Sets

Box Set 1 (Books 1-3)

Box Set 2 (Books 4-6)

Box Set 3 (Books 7-9)

Box Set 4 (Books 10-12)

Box Set 5 (Books 13-15)

Box Set 6 (Books 16-18)

Box Set 7 (Books 19-21)

Box Set 8 (Books 22-24)

Box Set 9 (Books 25-27)

Box Set 10 (Books 28-30)

Box Set 11 (Books 31-33)

Box Set 12 (Books 34-36)

Box Set 13 (Books 37-39)

Box Set 14 (Books 40-42)

Box Set 15 (Books 43-45)

Box Set 16 (Books 46-48)

Box Set 17 (Books 49-51)

Box Set 18 (Books 52-54)

The Mysteries of Max Big Box Sets

Big Box Set 1 (Books 1-10)

Big Box Set 2 (Books 11-20)

The Mysteries of Max Short Stories

Collection 1 (Stories 1-3)

Collection 2 (Stories 4-7)

Nora Steel

Murder Retreat

The Kellys

Murder Motel

Death in Suburbia

Emily Stone

Murder at the Art Class

Washington & Jefferson

First Shot

Alice Whitehouse

Spooky Times

Spooky Trills

Spooky End

Spooky Spells

Ghosts of London

Between a Ghost and a Spooky Place

Public Ghost Number One

Ghost Save the Queen

Box Set 1 (Books 1-3)

A Tale of Two Harrys

Ghost of Girlband Past

Ghostlier Things

Charleneland

Deadly Ride

Final Ride

Neighborhood Witch Committee

Witchy Start

Witchy Worries

Witchy Wishes

Saffron Diffley

Crime and Retribution

Vice and Verdict

Felonies and Penalties (Saffron Diffley Short 1)

The B-Team

Once Upon a Spy

Tate-à-Tate

Enemy of the Tates

Ghosts vs. Spies

The Ghost Who Came in from the Cold

Witchy Fingers

Witchy Trouble

Witchy Hexations

Witchy Possessions

Witchy Riches

Box Set 1 (Books 1-4)

The Mysteries of Bell & Whitehouse

One Spoonful of Trouble
Two Scoops of Murder
Three Shots of Disaster
Box Set 1 (Books 1-3)
A Twist of Wraith
A Touch of Ghost
A Clash of Spooks
Box Set 2 (Books 4-6)
The Stuffing of Nightmares
A Breath of Dead Air
An Act of Hodd
Box Set 3 (Books 7-9)
A Game of Dons

Standalone Novels
When in Bruges
The Whiskered Spy

ThrillFix
Homejacking
The Eighth Billionaire
The Wrong Woman

Printed in Great Britain
by Amazon